The A List

Launched to mark our forty-fifth anniversary, the A List is a series of handsome new editions of classic Anansi titles. Encompassing fiction, nonfiction, and poetry, this collection includes some of the finest books we've published. We feel that these are great reads, and the series is an excellent introduction to the world of Canadian literature. The redesigned A List books will feature new cover art by noted Canadian illustrators, and each edition begins with a new introduction by a notable writer. We can think of no better way to celebrate forty-five years of great publishing than by bringing these books back into the spotlight. We hope you'll agree.

Like This

Stories

Leo McKay Jr.

First published in 1995 by House of Anansi Press Ltd.

This edition published in 2014 by
House of Anansi Press Inc.
110 Spadina Avenue, Suite 801
Toronto, ON, M5V 2K4
Tel. 416-363-4343
Fax 416-363-1017
www.houseofanansi.com

Distributed in Canada by
HarperCollins Canada Ltd.
1995 Markham Road
Scarborough, ON, M1B 5M8
Toll free tel. 1-800-387-0117

Distributed in the United States by
Publishers Group West
1700 Fourth Street
Berkeley, CA 94710
Toll free tel. 1-800-788-3123

House of Anansi Press is committed to protecting our natural environment.
As part of our efforts, the interior of this book is printed on paper that contains 30%
post-consumer recycled fibres, is acid-free, and is processed chlorine-free.

18 17 16 15 14   1 2 3 4 5

Library and Archives Canada Cataloguing in Publication

McKay, Leo, Jr., 1964–, author
Like this : stories / Leo McKay Jr.

First published: Concord, Ont. : Anansi, 1995.
Issued in print and electronic formats.
ISBN 978-1-77089-833-2 (pbk.)—ISBN 978-1-77089-849-3 (html)

I. Title.

PS8575.K28747L54 2014   C813'.54   C2014-902692-7
                                        C2014-902693-5

Library of Congress Control Number: 2014938678

Cover design: Brian Morgan   Cover illustration: Michael Cho

We acknowledge for their financial support of our publishing program
the Canada Council for the Arts, the Ontario Arts Council, and the Government of Canada
through the Canada Book Fund.

Printed and bound in Canada

Introduction by Lynn Coady

Like This begins, appropriately enough, with a story about how adulthood begins. Meaning it's also a story about when childhood stops. On the surface, it's about three children who go off and play, but underneath, the story it tells is utterly primal, universal: the story of us all. There is the heat of high summer, a swollen river, a distracted and irritated mother shooing the youngsters out from her protective skirts and into the patiently waiting wilderness. Then there is the second wilderness, the one that exists within the prepubescent Angus, just as menacing, ". . . the other shade: black, damp and growing." The story, "Angus Fell," captures everything there is about the incalculable before-and-after of innocence lost — the terror but also the beauty, pushed unbearably close to one another.

The thread of the primal, the fundamental, runs through these eleven stories and cinches them together like a tightening fist. They are all as rough and as lovely as the rural and small-town Nova Scotia landscape in which they take place. Sometimes the roughness takes the upper hand, as in the gruff, heartbreaking title story, but Leo McKay is not the kind of writer who revels in human ugliness for its own sake — no matter how good he might be at rendering it. Young Cliff, raw from two weeks in detox, returns to his parents' home only to find himself fending off his blind-drunk father with a knife. The next morning is a brief, terrible set piece of despair and regret, in which McKay might have left his characters (and readers) wallowing if not for a sudden breakfast-table declaration on the father's part that gives the story a gut-wrenching twist of, yes, sadness but, unexpectedly — and gorgeously — hope.

In other instances, McKay's way with a simple, beautiful moment asserts itself, although the darkness is always there to temper the light. As Linda-Rose reflects in "The Ball," having been given a small flower by her suitor, "a rose only gets as big as it gets." That is to say that even though the story depicts a glorious instance in Linda-Rose's life, where her lover utterly proves himself worthy of her, the backdrop remains one of poverty, alcoholism, and her coal-miner father's blasted lungs. Yet it is the giddy buoyancy of the moment that infects the reader here — the darkness is briefly banished in favour of the joyful, incongruous image of a colourful beach ball being inflated before an enchanted child's eyes.

McKay's simple use of language is deceptive, can lull you into thinking these will be simple stories. But when the young teenage narrator of "Gold Wings" declares, "I was in America" as he walks away from his crumbling row-house neighbourhood into the moneyed subdivision on the other side of town, the layers of alienation and disenfranchisement buried in that straightforward subject, verb, preposition, and object — the fact that Valley View seems like a whole other world, a separate nation — lands like a punch in the gut. Furthermore, this is how McKay's characters both talk and think: in simple sentences that bob along on currents of unfathomable depth.

Leo McKay's Giller Prize-nominated work of stories showcases a young writer whose considerable gifts of nuance, tenderness, and fearlessness would eventually bring him such acclaim with his subsequent bestselling novel, *Twenty-Six*. McKay's seemingly effortless ability to depict the difficult and the ugly of life alongside all that is lovely and enduring, his eschewal of easy sentiment or easy answers, makes him an essential chronicler of contemporary Atlantic Canadian life — or, more simply put (in keeping with McKay's own style), a great Canadian writer.

This book is for Mum and Pop and Kathy and Joel

• CONTENTS

Angus woke at eight o'clock and noticed that for the first time since grade five had ended in the spring, there was no square of sunlight on the west wall of his bedroom. At the end of the hottest, driest summer anyone in Nova Scotia could remember, the clouds had closed in.

He rolled out of bed and stood before the open window. The sky was drained of colour. Out over the pointed roofs of the Red Row, the clouds were fat, dark, and dangerous. In the backyard, his mother's laundry flapped in the wind.

"Let's not go today," he called out the bedroom door to his brother, Tommy.

"Shut up," Tommy said. He ran across the hall in his underwear, an index finger over his lips.

"Go where?" Their mother called from downstairs. "Where do you two think you're going?"

Tommy glared at Angus and whispered, "Nice move, dummy."

"Nowhere, Mum," Tommy called down the stairs. "You know she's got ears like a hawk," he said to Angus. "C'mon and get dressed. Mary'll be here soon."

Downstairs, the wringer-washer foamed and churned. Their mother had the kitchen floor covered with dirty clothes, piled according to colour. She charged around the kitchen in a flowery sleeveless blouse. Her yellow nylon shorts barely circled her large belly, but hung baggy at her knees. Orange flip-flops snapped at her heels as she walked from piles of clothes to the washer beside the sink.

"You kids can get your own breakfast today," she said without looking up at them. "I've been up since six trying to get this laundry done before it rains."

Angus shook cornflakes into bowls for himself and his brother. As they sat at the table munching their cereal, their mother darted about the kitchen, filled a basket with wet clothes, then rushed out the door to the clothesline.

"Let's go bike riding instead," Angus said when she had gone. He didn't really want to go biking; it meant frustration and humiliation. Tommy was two years younger and considerably shorter than Angus, but he was trim and lithe and strong. Angus was thick around the middle. His shoulders were thin and narrow. Going biking with Tommy and Mary would mean trailing along behind them, exhausted and out of breath. But biking seemed the only alternative to going to the river.

"You a sissy or what?" Tommy said.

"It's gonna rain today," Angus said.

"So what?" Tommy said.

"The river gets big in the rain, it's dangerous."

"So if it rains we'll leave. Now quit whining, Mum'll hear and then she'll make us stay home."

"Good morning, Miss MacKenzie," their mother's voice came through the open window. "What are you selling this morning?"

"Oh, Mrs. Macintosh, you know I ain't selling nothing," came the reply.

The spring on the screen door creaked, then the door banged shut and Mary walked into the kitchen. Angus looked up from the table and smiled at her. She wore a white T-shirt and blue jeans. Her tanned skin was tight and smooth over the big bones of her face. A few large red freckles spotted her nose. When she smiled back at Angus, the contrast with her skin made her big, slightly crooked teeth look even bigger.

"Want some cornflakes?" Tommy said.

"Nope. Just had toast and tea," Mary said. She pulled out a chair and sat at the table between the two brothers.

"Angus doesn't want to go today," Tommy said. Mary looked at Angus. Angus lowered his eyes to his cereal.

"It *is* gonna rain," Mary said.

"So?" Tommy said.

"So maybe we could do something else," Mary said.

"We could go bike riding," Angus said. He looked at Mary.

"Forget it," Tommy said. He looked at the two of them defiantly. "I'm going. I don't care about you two." He stomped out the back door.

"Oh, I don't care. I don't care where we go," Mary said. She looked at Angus.

Angus shrugged. He got up from the table and followed Mary out the door.

"Where are you going?" their mother asked. She stood in a patchwork of flapping colours, her apron slung low around her waist. They didn't answer her.

Every morning she warned them not to go to the river. She didn't want them swimming without adult supervision. "I have no desire," she'd say, "to have to identify your dead bodies at the morgue, please and thank you." She also warned them about the men who lived on the riverbanks in summer. Angus, Tommy, and Mary had seen some of these men. *The drunkers,* they called them. The drunkers wandered the riverbanks, alone or in groups, quietly drinking until they found a shady place to pass out. Angus always got a sick feeling in his stomach when he saw the drunkers. They were dirty, hairy, old, and foul-mouthed. "God only knows what those men do besides wasting their lives away drunk," their mother said. "You two just stay clear of there. You hear me?" Angus and Tommy always lowered their heads or stared at the cereal box as she spoke.

They walked the same route today that they had walked every day of the summer: south through the Red Row and then east to the river. The lawns they walked across were brown and dead.

For Angus, the summer had had two starkly contrasting shades. On the outside it was sunny, hot, and dry. Dust coated the green reeds on the flood plain at the river. The dark silt in which the reeds grew was baked grey and rock hard. The sun had been unrelenting; it had beamed down on his head, bleaching his hair and making him dizzy by day's end.

Inside him was the other shade: black, damp, and growing. In the fall he would enter grade six, and things would change forever. Still, though he knew the changes were coming — could feel them at the heart of something deep within him — he didn't know what they would be. A new school, yes. New teachers. New things to learn, new things expected of him. In grade five at elementary school he had been one of the big kids, one of the oldest and biggest and wisest in the school. In the fall he would be small again.

But there was more to this darkness than school. All summer he had felt it. It had something to do with Mary, something to do with the shadow made by the golden hair growing on his body where it had never grown before.

Each day when he and Tommy and Mary reached the banks of the river, they peeled off their clothes. Angus and his brother swam in their white jockey shorts. In previous years Mary had swum in just her panties, but this year she also wore her undershirt. Angus had seen her bare skin all his life, at the river in the summer and on winter mornings when he would call for her before school. She'd come into the kitchen in her panties, drinking a cup of Red Rose tea. Her mother would help her get dressed and brush the tangles from her hair. This summer was different. She covered up. When she stepped from the rippling water, Angus could see what was happening, the sudden plumping of her chest.

Their swimming place was in front of a big drainpipe. The pipe collected water from all the manholes in town, surfacing in a grassy field near the river. Before the mouth of the pipe, a deep trench traced across the field to the flood plain. Where the grass ended at the edge of the trench, Angus, Tommy, and Mary would slide down the shaly bank to the bottom, using the trench as a pathway to the river.

There had been nothing from the drainpipe all summer — only the odd trickle when the town water truck made its rounds, rinsing dust and trash from the surfaces of roads. Today, under the dark sky, Angus wouldn't go into the trench. He stood at the top and walked along the edge as Tommy and Mary played below. Now and again he looked up to watch darker patches of clouds roll past.

He had seen the drainpipe in the spring when it had been bursting with murky water. The full, deep rushing sound the water had made, the powerfully churning brown surface; these had left Angus with an empty, trembly feeling in his chest. He had closed his eyes as he'd stood over the drowning banks and imagined himself below, struggling in vain against the current. Such a flood would leave anyone in its path helpless, pushing him to the river, and eventually, drowned, to the sea.

"Come on down," Tommy called from below. "It's not even raining. It'd have to pour all day to build up a current."

"Naw," Angus said, though he knew Tommy was right. Mary dug her strong hands into the earth and scrambled to the level of the grass Angus walked in. At the top, she swivelled her hips and skied on her sneaker heels back to the bottom of the trench. She let her hands and the bum of her jeans get dirty. She rubbed her dusty palms into her denim-covered thighs. Angus watched each assured motion of her body. He looked back to the gaping mouth of the pipe. Overhead, no sun shone through the thick clouds. He felt as though somewhere, in a place he couldn't see, a dam strained to keep from bursting.

At the edge of the field, where the trench met the flood plain, a weeping willow leaned out from the bank. The tree's roots broke from the earth beneath it, draping down to the level of the plain. Angus held onto the roots and lowered himself to the bottom. He ran through the dry reeds to catch up to Mary and Tommy, who were already at the water's edge.

They stripped down to their underwear and piled their clothes in heaps on the bank. Their skin was dark from a full summer spent in the sun. On both cheeks of Mary's bum, under the elastic leg band of her panties, stark lines showed, where golden brown skin turned white.

"Last one in's a rotten egg," said Tommy. He and Mary raced through the shallow water to their waists, where they plunged headlong into the sluggish current.

Angus rolled his socks into his sneakers. Mary and Tommy had almost reached the far bank as Angus walked into waist-deep water. The wind blew against his exposed body. A chill shook through him. The green, algae covered bottom felt slimy against his toes. He turned back and walked to shore.

"Where you going?" Mary called from the opposite bank.

"Too cold," Angus said.

"C'mon in," she said.

"Aw, leave him be," Tommy said.

Angus sat on a rock by the water's edge so he could dry off before putting his clothes back on. Tommy and Mary raced across the river toward him. When they got into the deepest water in the middle they stopped. "Let's see who can go farthest underwater," Tommy said.

"You always cheat," Mary said.

"Do not," Tommy said.

"Do so."

"Do not."

"Do so," Mary said. "Angus," she called. "Tommy does so always cheat, right?"

Angus pretended not to hear.

"You just know I always win, chicken," Tommy said.

Mary stood with her elbows above the current. She bounced up and down to keep warm. Angus knew she couldn't resist Tommy's challenge, especially since he'd called her chicken.

"All right, then," she said. "You go first."

Tommy took a big breath and dove in. While he was under the water, Mary turned to the bank and said, "Angus, you watch and make sure he doesn't cheat."

A few seconds later Tommy emerged downstream, gasping and panting. Mary gulped air and plunged below the surface. Tommy stepped slowly backwards as she approached him.

"You moved," Mary said when she surfaced.

"Did not," Tommy said.

Mary looked back toward Angus. Angus looked up at the sky.

"You were standing by that rock there when I went under," she said, pointing to a large boulder that rose above the surface of the water.

"I was not."

"Were too."

"Was not."

"Were too, and I'm not playing with a liar and a cheater no more." Mary turned her back on Tommy and walked toward the rocks where Angus sat.

Angus lowered his head as she approached.

Tommy was behind her saying, "See if I care. Just see if I care." He turned and swam for the opposite bank.

Mary's hair was plastered to her head and hung down in strings over her tanned shoulders. The white of her undershirt showed off her slim, taut muscles. The singlet was wet and slicked to her chest, showing her two little breasts.

"I'm not playing with cheaters no more," she said to Angus. He looked at her. Her lean torso made him ashamed of the way his own bulged out pudgy everywhere. She picked up a handful of rocks and pebbles and began tossing them one by one onto the flood plain behind him.

"Bet I can throw farther than you," she said.

"Probably," he said.

She sighed through her nose.

He shrugged.

"Race you to the bank," she said, nudging her head away from the river.

"Naw," said Angus.

"Aw, come off it, Angus," she said.

"I don't feel like it," he said. He sat with elbows on his knees, chin in his hands. She sat down to face him and mimicked his posture, pressing the rocks in her hand against her cheek. She clowned his grim face back at him. "Cut it out," he said.

"Cut it out," she said.

"Stop it," he said.

"Stop it," she said.

"Stop saying everything I say," he said.

"Stop saying everything I say," she said.

He crossed his arms over his chest and flopped them down against himself in frustration. "Stop making fun of me," he said.

Mary stood and pointed over Angus's shoulder. "Oh no, here come the drunkers," she said.

"What?" He jumped to his feet.

"Tricked you," Mary said. She pulled out the waistband of

Angus's undershorts and dropped in her handful of stones.

Angus cried out. The rocks were strange and warm from Mary's hand. He dug into his shorts and shook them to the ground. Mary laughed and ran past him.

Angus chased her across the flood plain. She scampered up the bank to the field beside the drainage ditch. He stumbled and clambered after her. Behind them Tommy called from the water. "Hey, where are you guys going?"

Mary waited until Angus got to the top of the bank, then started running again. He followed her through the tall grass, puffing and panting. She slowed, letting him come close. He reached out and grabbed the back of her panties. She swung wide and stopped, letting him fly past. He dragged her down with him when he fell.

They lay in the grass, laughing. They rolled around trying to get back on their feet. Mary was first to roll onto her hands and knees. As she was about to stand Angus pounced on her back. He knew her greatest weakness. He clamped his hands around her sides and dug his fingertips into her ribs. She bucked and howled and tried to throw him from her back. He let his weight flatten her to the ground and raked his fingers hard over her bones.

"No! No!" she screamed. She wailed helplessly, barely catching her breath as she laughed. She flopped from side to side, trying to free herself. It was no use. He had her pinned.

"I give, I give," she cried.

Her skin was smooth through the undershirt. He stopped tickling and lay quietly on top of her. The warmth of her body flooded through him. He leaned lower and put his face into the river-smell of her hair. From behind, he slid his hands flat across her chest. His throat seared dry. Neither of them made a sound. Her breathing swelled and deflated her chest against his hands. A hardness rose in his groin.

"What the fuck is going on here!" a coarse voice said.

Angus jumped to his feet, his heart pounding in his ears. A fat, hairy man stood knee-deep in the grass before him. He held a colourless bottle in one hand and was naked from the waist down.

Angus and Mary screamed and ran. Mary went in one direction, Angus another. He thumped and crunched across the field. Dry straw and rocks hurt his bare feet. Beneath his shorts, his erection flopped foolishly in front of him. He looked over his shoulder to see if the man was behind and the ground disappeared beneath him.

He skidded head first, on his elbows and knees, down the rough bank of the drainage ditch, bumping his head on a rock at the bottom.

He lay face down and bleeding. The black mouth of the drainpipe gaped over him. He could hear the man climbing down the bank. Angus whimpered and clutched his knees to his chest. The man set his bottle on the rocks with a clank. His scuffed black shoes stood out against his white ankles. A rough hand touched Angus's neck. "Was that your girlfriend?" the man said. He put his hand inside Angus's shorts. "Was that your girlfriend?" The hand slid across Angus's skin until it came to rest on his penis. "What were you doing with her?" His voice filled Angus's ear. On his breath was the sweet, sickening smell of alcohol.

"Don't be scared," the man said. "I just want to kiss your bum."

The man's hot erection was on Angus's thigh. Angus trembled and made a sound.

"I only want to kiss your bum," the man said.

Rain was falling lightly as Mary and Tommy climbed down the bank. They were dressed now, and had Angus's clothes for him. Angus had stopped crying. He lay curled on the rocks. Mary put her hand on his shoulder. "Are you okay?" she said.

He did not reply.

"Did he catch you?" said Tommy. "What did he say?"

Angus looked up at them. He shivered. Cold rain fell on his body. Mary and Tommy picked him up and helped him put on his clothes. He was smudged with dirt. Blood had started to congeal on his elbows and knees.

"Mum's going to take a fit when she sees you," Tommy said. "Don't tell we were at the river, Angus. Please don't tell we were at the river."

"Shut up," Mary snapped.

Angus said nothing.

"Angus, are you okay?" Mary said. "Can you walk home?"

He started to climb the bank, but he needed help to get up. At the top, he began limping slowly along the path toward home.

It was teeming rain by the time they got to their back door. Mary said goodbye. She said she hoped Angus would be all right.

"Jesus Christ!" their mother said. "Look at the two of you. Soaked to the arse. Not enough brains to come in out of the rain."

"But that's what we did," Tommy said.

"But that's what we did," their mother said.

Angus and Tommy stood dripping in the porch.

"Well, get those wet clothes off. Peel them off right there. You're not tracking up my house." She looked at Angus shivering and noticed his raw elbows. "What in the name of Jesus were you doing, Angus? Look at the mess of you."

Angus stood shivering and hugging himself. His teeth rattled.

"Angus fell," Tommy said.

"*Angus fell,*" their mother said.

Angus slowly peeled off his clothes and left them in the porch. The kitchen, strung with the drab colours of wet laundry, looked like a sad, rained-out circus.

He limped naked to the bathroom, his arms clasped tightly around himself. His mother ran a bath. Thick bubbles floated on the water. Steam rose around her head as she leaned over to shut off the tap. He stood there bloody and dirty and wet.

"Look at you. Just look at you," she said. She examined his scraped elbows and knees and clucked her tongue. She rolled up some toilet paper, doused it with rubbing alcohol, and dabbed at his abrasions. Angus winced, but did not make a sound.

"You take a long, hot soak in that tub," his mother said. "And make sure you scrub behind those ears." When she walked out, Angus locked the door. He turned his back to the mirror over the sink. He did not want to look at himself.

He stepped into the steaming water. It burned his skin. The places where he was chafed and raw hurt worst.

He sank into the bubbles as he sat down. He lay back and let the heat envelop him, only his eyes and mouth above the surface of the water. The warm rush of sounds in his ears comforted him. Bubbles closed around his face, quivering with each breath he took.

That night the rain rattled off his window as he lay in bed, sleeping, waking, dreaming. His mother came in to see him the next morning.

"Not feeling too good?" she said softly. She sat on the edge of the bed.

"No," he said. He opened his mouth as though he were about to say something. His mother put her hand to his forehead. "No fever," she said.

He made a noise.

His mother looked at him.

He wanted to tell her. He wanted the words inside him to be big, smooth stones he could slide over his tongue and onto the bedclothes. He wanted his mother to gather the words in her apron and take them away forever. But instead of stones, the words were balls of barbed wire. They stuck in the soft flesh of his throat when he tried to speak.

"I hate to see you sick," his mother said. "But you have to learn to come in out of the rain."

All day he lay in bed — awake, asleep. It rained and rained outside. His mother brought him cups of Campbell's soup. He drank these slowly, and now and again he got up to go to the bathroom.

Tommy stayed downstairs all day, playing with Lego. Angus imagined the bright, solid colours of the blocks as he heard them pop apart, and then back together. In the afternoon, Tommy came into his room.

"What happened yesterday, Angus?" he asked. "Did you let that drunker catch you?"

Angus shrugged at him.

"You're not going to tell, are you?" Tommy said.

Angus rolled over to face the wall.

The next morning was sunny. Angus got up at six, while everyone else in the house was still asleep. He went out the back door and headed for the river. It was too early for the drunkers; they would still be hiding wherever they hid from the rain. Even so, Angus kept one hand in his pocket, on the paring knife that he'd taken from the kitchen.

The river was swollen and violent. It covered the flood plain. He stood over the column of water that rushed out of the pipe. Below him, the trench was flooded. The banks were already noticeably wider. The rocks with his blood on them had been washed away.

He edged the toes of his sneakers to the lip of the pipe and leaned out over the current. The water smelled like rusty iron.

He closed his eyes, and for an instant saw himself from far above. At first he was like a tiny blip on a radar screen. Then he got larger, grew legs, sprouted arms — metamorphosed like a frog in a pond. He saw himself fully grown: arms, legs, the features of his face. Eyes closed.

He leaned farther over the water, tipped forward, fell. The current was swift and sucked him down quickly. He twisted and smashed against rocks at the bottom. He opened his eyes in the murkiness and was blind. His legs swirled in the churning current. His head bobbed abruptly to the surface, and he choked and spit mouthfuls of dirty water. He rolled over and crashed into the dirt where the banks narrowed toward the river. He clawed frantically at the ground and grabbed at rocks and branches as he slid along the bank. Stones bit into his hands. He tried to dig his feet into the bottom. His head went under.

He gulped water, felt his shoulder hit something. It rolled him lengthwise to the surface. The bank rushed past. He gouged it with his hands. Soil and stones came loose in his fingers. He slipped deeper into the current. He choked and gasped, trying to keep his head in the air. Again he went under.

He swallowed water and mud, smashed against rocks. Broke the surface and gasped for breath. Grey spray and dirt. The roar of the river. His hands fumbled and clawed. Rocks and dirt and clumps of weeds. A tree overhead. A patch of blue. In his palm, something solid. A root. He tightened his fist.

The current tried hard to loosen him from where he was fastened. But he worked his other arm out of the water and grasped a root higher up the bank. He pulled himself up, grasped another root, lifted himself again until only his feet remained in the water. Above him, the branches of the willow looked black against the morning sky. He pressed a cheek against the ground and vomited muddy water and blood.

• LIKE THIS

It's the Old Man again. Giving me shit. Things was bad enough to start with, what with me leaving school and all, but two weeks out of the detox and he comes home last night drunk. That's all I needed.

Mum and me was watching the night-time *Wheel of Fortune*. We had the screen door on the back hooked to keep it from banging in the wind. We heard him and his pounding, but before either of us could get there, he put his hand through the mesh and unhooked it himself. "Mary, mother of Christ," he says.

"Frank," Mum says. "Frank, there's no need of this."

"Jesus Christ," he says. He staggers from the porch into the kitchen.

"Frank," Mum says. "Frank, it's raining out. You're tracking mud on the floor."

"I pay the bills in this shack," he says. "I pay the goddam bills." In the dark kitchen he stands in the light coming out of the fridge. He takes a piece of Polish sausage from the meat drawer.

Mum switches on the light.

"Frank, please take off your boots," she says. "Frank, please. I just waxed that floor."

"I'll burn the son-of-a-whore down," he says. "I'll burn her to the goddam ground." He goes to the stove and turns a knob. He sticks the sausage in a pot of water. He spills water on the floor as he sets the pot on the burner. I stand in the doorway, watching. The pot begins to hiss.

"Frank, please. You're making a mess," says Mum.

"I'll make you a mess," he says. "I'll show you what kinda mess I can make." He sways back to the fridge and pulls the doily off the top. Bananas, pens, pencils, note-paper, nickels and dimes, and a ceramic frog crash to the floor. The frog breaks. I remember that frog. It used to be my piggy-bank.

"Aw, Frank," says Mum. "Frank," she says. "Don't start, okay?" She puts her hand on his shoulder. He takes a swing at it, knocks it away. He takes another swing, hits her. Across the face. I've seen worse.

"Aw, Frank," she says. "Frank, don't be like this."

He has his back turned now. He sticks a fork in at the sausage. She comes up behind him and puts her hand on his shoulder again.

"Did you have your supper?" she says. "I'll make you supper. Are you hungry? You just take off your workboots and go in and watch TV. I'll get your supper for you."

"Get the Jesus away from me," he yells. He turns around

and shoves her. She stumbles backwards. Her head smacks the wall, then she slides to the floor.

I can't take no more of this. I go to the drawer under the counter and pull out the butcher knife.

He takes a step toward me, then stops.

I hold the knife in both hands and point it at him. "Get the fuck out of here," I say, but I say it too loud. I wanted to sound serious, but it come out scared. I jab the blade at him, then at the door. "Get out."

Mum's on her feet now, and me and the Old Man square off. He looks pretty far gone. He shakes his head, but I don't know what that means.

"Oh Jesus, Cliffy," Mum says. "Oh Jesus, sweet Jesus."

"Just stay back, Mum," I say. But she knows to stay back.

"What the fuck do you think you're doing?" the Old Man says. He blinks like he can't see too good. He's still shaking his head.

"Turn around out that door and get out," I say. I try to stay calm. I keep the knife out in front of me, and we slowly circle each other.

"Oh Jesus, Cliffy," Mum says. "Jesus, sweet Jesus."

"Mum, shut up," I say. I try to concentrate. I try to see what he'll do. "Shut up, please."

She starts whispering to herself, "Jesus, holy Jesus."

"You put that knife down," the Old Man says.

"We've had e-fucking-nough of you," I say. "Get out."

We circle.

"You put that fucking thing away from me in *my* house," he says. He's got this crazy smile on his face. I'm sorry I ever picked up the knife. I should have got my hockey stick from the porch. I should have bashed him on the head with the kettle.

He hunkers down and dives for me. I point the knife away from the both of us, and he grabs me at the shoulders, wrestling.

"You little bastard," he says. He grunts and pushes. He pulls at my elbow with his bad hand, and the knife flashes between our faces. I yank it back fast and it cuts me under the nose.

I put the knife up over my head to get it away from us. He gets more frantic. He thinks I'm going to come down with it. He pushes me to the wall and shoves me again and again against it. I feel my cut nose bleeding. His shoulder pushes into my face. My blood is smeared on his blue broken heart tattoo. We're both reaching up for the knife. It waves over us, back and forth.

I try to get my arm free. I want to throw the knife clear. He makes little screams in his throat as he slams me and slams me into the wall.

I try to free my arm. We reach up. The knife is way up there. The tip digs into the ceiling tiles.

He bangs my wrist against the wall. Bangs it and bangs it till I don't think I can hold on to the knife any longer.

Then I hear this crack.

He lets out one scream and steps back. He puts his hands to his head.

The knife clangs to the floor. I jump and come down hard, real hard, with the heel of my foot on the instep of his. He bends over slowly, mouth open. When he lifts his foot to his hands, he tips over backwards without a peep. On the way down, his head bounces off the glass window in the oven door.

That's the end of him. For this night.

Mum is standing back of where the Old Man fell. She's

got the big, one-handled cutting board in her hands. Her eyes are full of tears, but she's got her jaw set. I know she don't want to cry.

She looks down at the Old Man and says, "Oh Frank, Frank. What are we going to do?"

At that moment, the pot of water and sausage boils over onto the burner.

This morning it's like nothing happened. Everybody goes out of their way to act normal. Except my nose is taped up, and the Old Man is sitting at the table with one workboot on. He can't get it off. The foot I stomped last night is too swole-up. He had to cut one leg out of a pair of pyjamas just to put them on.

"Could I have some more coffee, please?" he says to Mum. Please. Imagine.

Mum does her best to go along with it. "Would anyone like another egg?" she says.

I heard her phone the Car Works earlier to tell them the Old Man wasn't coming in. "No, it's nothing like that, Sonny," she said. That foreman knows her pretty good. "He's got a foot that's paining him something merciful." At least she didn't have to lie.

I keep my face in my Shreddies as we eat. I try to stay out of things. The Old Man is pretty quiet too, at first. He swishes the coffee around in his cup. He scrunches his head down and brings his shoulders up, like his head's not attached and he's got to balance it there on his neck. He looks at us with his eyes half closed. He knows he done something bad, but he can't remember what it was. We remember. He knows that.

I heard him first thing — even before I heard Mum on the phone — barfing and ralphing his guts up in the toilet.

Outside it's sunny. Through the living room and out the front window we can see kids from the neighbourhood pass by on their way to school. I'm sitting there in an old pair of shorts and a T-shirt.

"You're gonna be late," he says to me.

I knew this was coming. I don't say nothing.

He makes a nod at the clock over the table. "You're gonna be late."

"You know, man," I say.

"I don't know shit," he says. "You're gonna be late for school."

"You know I ain't going back there," I say.

"What you gonna do then?" he wants to know.

"I don't want to talk about it. Especially with you."

"Look," he says.

"I already talked to every teacher and their fucking dog up there," I say.

"Look," he says, louder than he's said anything this morning. "There's stuff them teachers don't know."

"Tell me about it," I say.

"That ain't what I'm talking about," he says.

He gets up from his chair and stands in the centre of the floor. He puts his arms out. First I think he wants to fight again. But he's sober today. He's played out.

I put my head back to my cereal.

"Look, you little son-of-a-whore," he says. "Look!"

When I look up again, he says something. He says, "You tell me if you want to end up like this."

He holds his hands out from his sides. I look at his bad hand. The one that's only a thumb. The one that got sheared off in a big set of metal shears at work ten years ago. With a hand like that, you hold it out, a person thinks that's what you're talking about. But he just looks at me.

He needs a shave. He's got no teeth. Big circles loop beneath his eyes. He stands there in an undershirt with one workboot on and one leg cut out of a pair of pyjamas, trying to keep his head balanced on his shoulders.

Mum looks at the Old Man like she never saw him before. Like she was surprised to find him there first thing in the morning, hung over and missing work. She looks at him a while, then turns to me.

I put my head down and take another spoonful of Shreddies.

Mum refills the Old Man's cup. "You ought to take the weight off that hurt foot, Frank," she says. The Old Man sits back down.

• THE BALL

I told him yes.

I was on my hands and knees in the garden, thinning out the lettuce. I had an old plaid dress on and my apron over it. He had on them pleated pants I sometimes see he wears to Mass. They was the first things I saw there between the splatters of whitewash on the backs of the fence pickets. I stood up tall and skinny as I am and he was taller and skinnier.

It was seven o'clock at night with the sun just ready to tip off the peak of Perley Baudoux's store and roll down the other side out of sight. And me with work in the morning.

His hair was trimmed nice and neat, and the way he gave me that look he gives me, looking his sort of bad eye around the little hill in the middle of his nose and them dark dark eyebrows pushed down over his eyes, I never thought the word beautiful could be used for a boy before. In his case a man by now. But that's what I was thinking. You are beautiful. Beautiful, beautiful, beautiful. But I never said nothing.

I had said give me a week and I guess it had just about been a week. Just about exactly, but I thought of it as more of a weekend thing. More of a Sunday afternoon thing, what with both of us working. Truth be told I thought if he had waited five years already he could wait a few more days. But here it was Wednesday and here he was there.

Over the fence he passed me a small pinkish wild rose and looked beyond my shoulder to where the sunflowers stood tall and without movement against the house. He looked at them for a minute. Maybe he thought that rose was awful small in comparison. It was. A rose only gets as big as it gets, that's what I say.

He reached his wide hand to my shoulder and leaned me a sharp peck on the face. I could feel me turn red. I pointed him to the back door and walked the two-by-six path through the potatoes to meet him there. On the back step he snuck his arm around the apron strings on my waist and pecked me another good one.

I could see the arse of a bottle poke out from under his jacket. I knew what he was up to.

"How do you say 'dad' in Russian?" he said.

"All I know is *shruka*," I said. "That means arse-hole."

He laughed and laughed and threw back his head. He tried to peck me again, but I made for the door. "I guess you better come in," I said.

Daddy was right there. Sitting in the porch by the coal scuttle smoking his makens. He had his rocker going. "Jeese

Christ," he said. He knew who it was all right. But he didn't know what was going on.

"Scott. For love of Christ." Somewhere under the bib of my apron there was something went sproing. Something that said maybe Daddy would get up. Maybe he would pick up that broad-lipped coal shovel from behind him and flatten Scott's dark beautiful head.

Maybe five years ago. Not now.

"Look what I brung you, there, Joe. Some of that good bo-hunk whiskey." Scott slipped the bottle from under his coat. It was vodka.

Daddy drinks rum himself. Vodka gives him the shakes. "Jeese Christ," he said. "Goddam, no good, son of bitch of wudka."

Scott laughed.

I shook my head at Daddy. Through his pop bottle glasses he gave me a look. We all went into the kitchen. I took down two tall mustard jar glasses from the cupboard. Scott and Daddy mixed vodka and tap water in them and sat at the table. "Linda-Rose," said Scott. "Pour some for your own-self."

"No way," I said. I never drink but tea and water. He knows that.

"She don't drink," said Daddy.

"She don't drink," said Scott. He swished his vodka around in his glass. He took a sip. Daddy did too.

I took this little pudding bowl and half filled it with water. I cut the flower from the stem of the wild rose and dropped it in the bowl. Then I turned around.

From where I stood, with my bum to the sink, the doorway to the living room flickered blue. The TV was going in there. I saw Scott peeking around to get a look.

"TV's going," I said. I bumped my bum into the sink a couple times.

"Ya." He had this tone to his voice. He poked his head up again and looked in. His face flickered in the blue light coming through. We heard Fred Flintstone. "Wilma! I'm home." Dino barked, if that's what Dino is supposed to do. He's a dinosaur. "Wilma. Wilma? *Wilma!*"

"You still on at plant?" Daddy said.

"Yup," said Scott. He sat back and rubbed his wide hand over his brushcut. "Some guys down there like the work. Some guys don't like it. Me, I don't think about it one way or the other. As far as work goes, it's work. Put it that way." He took another drink.

Daddy looked at his vodka.

I went to the table and sat on a chair between the two of them.

"Scott's big in the union down there," I said. My friend Loretta Sarson from the dairy, her husband Mike works down the Car Works. Loretta told me Mike told her Scott was a shop steward. Steward or Stewart. We don't have a union at the dairy.

Daddy looked right at Scott as if he figured Scott might have something else to say.

Scott made a face. "I don't know. I like to help out is all."

Daddy never said nothing.

"You got one person," said Scott. He shook his hands out in front of him. "Well that one person, there ain't much they can do is there? It's just one person, right. Well you put that one person together with one more person. Then that's something else. That's a whole new ballgame is what it is."

A commercial started up on the TV. Ivory soap. That TV was up pretty loud. We all sat there in the sound it made.

Some woman and her husband. Him talking about her face.

When Fred Flintstone came back on there was a laugh. It came from the blue flickering room. It was high and little. More of a squeal than a laugh. Still, there was no pretending. The three of us at the kitchen table looked at each other.

"Lord save us," I said. "Where's my manners?" I went to the cupboard. "I got biscuits. I got peanut butter cookies. I got a loaf of yesterday's bread. Are you hungry at all, Scott?"

"No. No. Thanks," he said. He might have been looking right at Daddy. He wasn't, though. He was looking into the room.

"I got Jello in the fridge," I said. "Don't got no whip-cream but there's milk. That's the way I like mine. Just some milk on it."

"No. Thanks. I already et."

The Flintstones music came on. I couldn't see, but I knew Fred was getting locked out of the house by the cat. "Wilma!" he yelled. We heard him pounding on the door.

Then Stephie came in. She stood in the doorway with the blue light flickering behind her. She had on her pink nightie and the red, white, and pink slippers I crocheted for her last winter. I had already given her her bath and she stood there bright as a spark, her hair hanging down in ringlets.

"I never heard nobody out here," she said. She peeked up shy at Scott. He had his chin on his chest and was peeking down the same way at her. Daddy sat and watched the whole thing.

I opened my arms and she ran across the oilcloth into them. I picked her up and she hugged my neck. "Mama," she whispered in my ear. "Mama, Fred Flintstone is funny."

I bounced her a couple times like when she was a baby. Then I set her on the floor.

Scott opened his mouth and some strange noise came out. Some kind of squawk or cough. He cleared his throat. Then he said, "Hi, Stephie." He bent way over in his chair and looked across at her. Stephie held on to my leg, right shy.

"This here's Scott," I said. I didn't know what else to say. "He's Mama's friend," I said, and left it at that.

Scott looked up at me, then over to Daddy. "Come here till I show you something," he said to Stephie. "I got a surprise."

She stood and looked at him. He reached into his jacket pocket and pulled something out. It was small and puckered and plastic, and he dangled it out in front of him. "See?" he said.

Stephie held tighter to my leg.

"Watch," said Scott. He took the thing and blew into it. It got bigger. He blew into it some more. It's a good thing he isn't a miner. Daddy couldn't have blew that thing up supposing he tried all day. It was a beach ball. Big and round and red and white and blue.

He held it out.

Stephie moved toward it. She spread her arms wide and took it from Scott. It was nearly as big as her. It swayed over her like a funny head. It was all she could do just to keep her grip.

She jumped up a couple times like she was testing how heavy it was. Then she ran with it. She couldn't see where she was going and she ran right into Daddy's chair. The ball bounced her back and she changed direction. This time she ran into Scott's knees. She turned and made a beeline for the cupboards. Thump! She bumped right into them, bounced away, and landed on her bum. The ball rolled across the floor.

We all laughed.

I told him yes.

• GOLD WINGS

I remember the first time I saw Paul Semple's father's motorcycle. It was a Sunday late in the summer that I turned fifteen. A week later, I saw the motorcycle again. Something terrible happened in the space of those seven days. Terrible.

On the last night of summer, the night before the first day of school, Kevin McPhadden and I were hanging out on Foord Street, the main street in town. We leaned back against the glass storefront of Superior Fuels, watching the cars go by. We stood and sat on the concrete steps for hours, from early in the afternoon until the sun had almost set. We'd sit down and watch the cars go by, spitting down between our feet onto the sidewalk. When our feet went to sleep, we'd stand up, shake out our legs, and use the height we'd gained to spit clear across the sidewalk, over the curb, and onto the street. Cars passed slowly, full of people we didn't know. Now and then a car pulled into the Quik Pik across from us and the driver got out. We'd watch through the big front window as the driver wandered around inside the store, eventually getting back into the car and driving off.

By the time the shadow of Stedman's department store had passed across the street, eclipsing the sun, Kevin and I had darkened a wide slice of sidewalk and a small half-moon of road pavement with our spit. The sky was the dark, cold blue of a summer emptied of heat. Clouds trickled past overhead like water in a slow stream.

As I thought about returning to school the next day, I remembered having left school in June — the way I'd felt. I remembered leaving class and going out the front door into the schoolyard with an armload of dog-eared notebooks. I had walked to the far side of the yard to a garbage can at the edge of the basketball court. I pushed back the lid of the can, letting it swing back and forth a couple of times while I hoisted the notebooks to my shoulder. Then I jammed the stack of scribblers into the garbage. I sighed, dusted my hands, and went home. The whole summer had lain ahead of me.

"Maybe I won't go back," Kevin said suddenly. He looked away from me as he said it. He looked down the street to the south. He spat another dot onto the sidewalk.

"Home?" I said. A car with no muffler sped past, leaving a long cloud of blue smoke hanging over the street.

"What?" Kevin said. He looked at me.

"Go back where?" I said. "Home?" I knew a few things

about Kevins life at home, and I would not have blamed him if he didn't want to go back there. I knew, for instance, that Kevin had seventeen brothers and sisters, and that most of them lived at least part of the time at home. They lived in a Red Row house, an old mining company house exactly like mine. At Kevin's place, twenty people shared the same amount of space I often complained was too small for my parents, my kid brother, and me.

Out behind the McPhadden house were two early seventies model Chev Impalas, big wide boats of cars. The only thing wrong with these cars was that they didn't run. They had seized up from disuse. Each night from mid-May to October, a red and black wool blanket wrapped about him, Kevin made his bed in one or the other of the cars. "It's lonely out there," he told me one day. "But I like it. Nice soft seats to sleep on, radio. Too crowded indoors anyways." When the night was clear he slept in the faded blue Impala, because the battery was not yet dead, and he could listen to CKEC Radio in New Glasgow. When it rained he slept in the dark blue, because the windows rolled up tighter.

Kevin narrowed his eyes, thinking about what I'd asked. "Not go back home," he said. "That's not a bad idea." He shook his head and looked back up the street. "School," he said. "Shit."

"School," I said. "What would you do?"

He turned back to look at me. He had a long, thin scar that ran from under his hairline to the corner of one eyebrow. The way the light had started to dim made the scar stand out white. "Anything," he said. "I'd do anything."

Across the street Paul Semple, a guy my age, came out of an alley and went through the front door of the Quik Pik.

"Not that asshole," Kevin said. We watched as Semple passed up and down the narrow aisles of the Quik Pik.

"He's not so bad," I said. "He's all right."

"You can't believe a word that guy says," Kevin said.

"So," I said. "I don't. I don't believe a word."

There is a name for people like Paul Semple, people who make things up. I knew the name even when I was fifteen. I'd learned it from a magazine article I'd read: pathological liar. Although he lived in Valley Woods, "The County's Premier Subdivision," as the sign assured the people who lived there, Paul never seemed satisfied with his life as it really was. Given the chance, he would exaggerate any story out of shape, or else he'd make a new story up fresh, right off the top of his head.

Paul came out of the Quik Pik sucking on a bottle of pop. He stood on the sidewalk, looked up at us, and smiled.

"Oh, Jesus," Kevin said.

Paul loped in long strides to our side of the street. "Jesus, Jesus," Kevin said.

"Shut up," I said. I elbowed Kevin.

"Hey, boys," Paul said when he reached us. He smiled in a silly way and bobbed his head up and down. "Not home sharpening up those pencils?"

"Already got them sharpened," I said. I held out my hand.

He put the bottle in my palm. Spitting all afternoon had dried my mouth. I took a long drink.

When I lowered the bottle, Paul took it back and said, "You want some?" He looked into the space between Kevin and me. Kevin twitched his head toward his shoulder.

Paul balanced on his toes on the edge of the concrete step and kept the silly smile on his face. He rocked back and forth and started talking. He had a loud, strong voice and he liked to use it. He talked about the school year that was about to begin. He told us that he already knew what homeroom he'd be in because he'd broken into the school and fished the information out of a filing cabinet in the principal's office.

"Bullshit," Kevin said. He started kicking the ground with his feet.

I elbowed him. I knew the story was a lie as well as he did, but I didn't see any point in contradicting it. Paul would only insist all the more that it was true.

"Care to place a bet?" Paul challenged. He held his hand out to Kevin and looked into his face. "There's a photocopy of the class list on the desk in my bedroom. I can show you anytime. I can also tell you what class *you're* in, McPhadden, if you care to know."

Kevin was getting edgy, eager to take Paul up on his bet. I put myself firmly between the two of them and said: "We'll all find out tomorrow. I'd hate to spoil the surprise." Then I started laughing, and even though it was a fake laugh, it seemed to take the edge off the situation. Kevin settled down a little. His feet stopped shuffling against the ground.

Paul stood down from the edge of the step. He relaxed a little and slouched against the side of the door frame we were standing in. It wasn't long before he was talking about the motorcycle his father had bought the day before. It was a Gold Wing, he said. A seven-fifty. It had chrome this and chrome that. He said his father had bought it from an ex-Hell's Angel who was now selling bikes in Halifax.

We listened to Paul go on about the bike for a few minutes, neither of us saying much. Then Kevin said, "How's your old man getting this bike home from Halifax?"

"He took it back in a truck he borrowed from work," Paul said.

"Already here is it?"

"Yes. It is."

"In town?"

"Yes."

"I suppose your old man is out for a nice long ride on a day like today."

"He's working today. He works Sundays," Paul said.

"I see. Took the bike to work, did he? Wants to show it off to his friends?"

"He doesn't want to leave it in the parking lot for eight hours," Paul said. "It isn't safe."

"Sure," Kevin said. "It isn't safe."

"It's not," Paul said. Then, looking only at me, he said: "You want to see it?"

"Sure," I said.

Paul looked at Kevin. "You coming too?" he asked halfheartedly.

Kevin knew that a lot of parents didn't like their kids hanging around with him. Some of his brothers had been in jail, and the McPhadden name was not a good one to have in town. He would usually save a kid the embarrassment of bringing him home — and himself the embarrassment of not being invited — by refusing outright to visit anyone's house.

"I'm going," Kevin said. "You bet I am."

Valley Woods was the kind of neighbourhood the Brady Bunch lived in. I had seen Valley Woods plenty of times before, but always from the back end: picnic tables, clotheslines, lawn mowers, jungle gyms. There was a path that led from the elementary school in town, through a stand of woods, to a small clearing on a hill. Beyond this clearing the path continued through a gully, across a brook, and into Valley Woods itself, but I had never taken the path that far. On the weekends during the summer a gang of us would take the path to the clearing, where we'd sit on fallen trees and drink beer. After dark you'd see lights come on in people's kitchens, a passing outline of someone's head. That day, though, with Paul leading the way, we entered Valley Woods from the front end. We saw carports and hedges, wrought iron railings, paved driveways.

My father had always told me I was a Canadian but that all the places I saw on TV were American. I guess as a kid the differences you see are the obvious ones. But as we walked past the low, modern houses of Valley Woods, I was in America. At the other end of town, in the Red Row, the neighbourhood Kevin and I lived in, the houses were tall and old and pointed, company houses from the mining days. Sure, I had been in rich neighbourhoods around the county before. Maybe it would be Christmas and my family would be looking at the lights. But the world looks different from inside a car. It's a lot like TV, seeing things pass by on the other side of that windshield. When you walk, you move slowly. You see things. I remember wondering what Kevin was thinking as we walked into Valley Woods.

It stood gleaming in the driveway, the proof of its own existence. Paul ran ahead so he could sit on it while we watched. Kevin was right behind me, and I heard him let out the smallest sound at the sight of it. Neither Kevin nor I knew anything about bikes, and neither of us spoke as Paul went through the same description he had given us on the main street. We didn't need it now. Words only cheapened the glory we felt in standing next to such a machine. The gas tank and a small triangular cover plate on each side were silken, unblemished red. The last rays of light from the sky glinted off the chrome. Paul settled onto the seat and crouched down, as though to slice through wind.

"Let me sit on it," I said.

Paul got up. I sat on the seat and twisted the throttle. I made a motorcycle noise. I leaned forward and looked up over the handlebars and across the backyard. I thought of power, and of going places.

"You'll flood it," Paul said.

"Sorry," I said. I let go of the throttle and sat up straight. "Cool bike," I said.

"You want to sit on it?" Paul asked, looking straight at Kevin.

Kevin was staring at his shoes. "You sick?" he said. He made a move toward the street with his head. "You coming?" he asked me.

I looked at Paul.

He shrugged.

"Yeah, sure," I said. "I guess I should be getting home." I got off the bike.

Paul stood in the driveway as we left. When we reached the road I looked back and noticed his mother in the front window, looking out at Kevin and me. She met Paul at the door as he went in.

It was a week later, on Sunday, that Paul Semple phoned me. It was dusk, and when the phone rang I was standing at the screen door at the back of our house, watching the sun set over the hills to the west of town.

I heard my mother get up from the couch in the living room and go into the kitchen. "Hello," she said. Then she called my name.

"You seen Kevin today?" Paul wanted to know.

"No. I haven't seen him since . . ." I thought for a moment. "Wednesday." He hadn't been in school Thursday or Friday.

"We went to his house, but he wasn't there," Paul said. "We asked his mother when she'd seen him last, but all she said was, 'A while ago.'"

Someone had stolen the dream machine. The Semples had gone to bed the night before, and when they woke up it was gone. There wasn't much the police could do. They interviewed the neighbours, but nobody had seen or heard anything.

At supper time, the Campbells, the Semples's nextdoor neighbours, arrived home from a day at the beach. Mrs. Campbell worked the four to twelve shift at the Michelin plant in Granton. She told Paul's father she'd been coming home from work at about one in the morning when she'd seen Kevin walking up the street in the direction of the Semple house. She'd thought at the time to phone the police, she said. But she remembered having seen Kevin in the Semple's driveway the week before.

"What are you saying?" I asked Paul.

"We're not saying anything," Paul said.

"I don't think he knows how to drive a bike," I said.

"Dad says even if he didn't take it, maybe he saw who did."

"Aw, cripes," I said. I felt my heart sink to a place deep inside me.

I hung up the phone. My mother was sitting at the table with a cup of tea. "What's wrong?" she asked.

"Nothing," I said. I took a banana from the top of the fridge and sat down across from her. As I ate I thought about Kevin. On the way home from Valley Woods the week before, that bike was all I'd talked about. How cool it was. How fast it would go. Kevin had told me to shut up about it.

I threw the empty peel into the garbage can by the stove and walked outside for the first time that day. My mother called after me to put on a jacket.

People hadn't closed the curtains on their front windows yet, and as I walked from the Red Row to Valley Woods, I looked shamelessly in at them as they sat in front of their televisions. Fat, middle-aged men and women and their kids. The blue light from the TVs made them look as if they'd come from a planet unknown to me. Kids not much younger than I was were already in pyjamas, watching the end of *The Wonderful World of Disney*. Women stood over sinks, washing supper dishes. Men watched the last football game of the weekend. By the time I reached Valley Woods the light was gone from the sky. Night had fallen completely. The curtains were closed in the windows of the houses I passed.

There was movement behind the curtains of the Semple house. The floodlight over the driveway seemed a memorial to the lost motorcycle. I stood only a moment. I was conscious that I was from the Red Row, and people would be on the lookout, now that something had gone wrong.

I walked up the street and turned down a footpath I thought must be the one that led north to the clearing where my friends and I drank. Kids from Valley Woods used the path every day through the week, but on the weekends their parents told them to stay away from it. They'd heard the teenagers drinking there.

The path was dark, but the moon was coming up through the trees in the east. The smell is what I noticed, the smell of trees and earth. The ground was springy beneath my feet. I smelled the needles of pine and spruce.

A swath of stars, fading as the moonlight increased, dipped through the trees overhead. I followed the path downhill to a place where it turned sharply to the left and crossed a brook. At the top of the rise on the other side of the brook would be the clearing. Alder bushes grew at the bottom of the gully. I reached the mossy bank of the brook and stopped, putting my weight on my front foot to jump to the opposite side. Standing poised to jump, with my arms out from my sides for balance, I took in a breath. There was a strange smell in the air. A dull, metallic smell, stronger than the smell of nature. Gasoline.

I peered into the woods on either side of the path I was following. Something looked strange back where I'd turned, something I hadn't noticed when I'd gone past. White flesh of broken alder branches showed against the black shadows of leaves.

I went back to the bend in the path and looked straight into the woods, straight where you'd go if you didn't turn when the path did. The alder branches were broken and pushed away where something had gone through. I saw a glint of chrome in the moonlight.

The bike lay on its side in the brook. The water wasn't deep enough to cover it, but its gas tank was half-submerged. Moonlight reflected off a blue gasoline rainbow on the water's surface. A scorch mark blackened the chrome below the gas tank, where a little fire had burned, then gone out.

I jumped across the water to the opposite bank. Kevin lay face down at the base of a thick spruce. His arms were at his sides deliberately, the way a fifteen-year-old boy will hold his arms while he stands on someone's doorstep after walking her home from the dance. He doesn't want to stand too close to her. She might get angry. And he doesn't yet know what to do with hands.

He shifts his weight from one foot to the other. He makes a silly joke. She laughs nervously. Inside him are the sharp spikes of terror, but he knows that all he must do is ride out this moment. In the end she will stand quietly and look at him. He will take one step toward her, and their lips will briefly meet. On the way home, he will smile like a man drunk on oxygen, stumbling over cracks in the sidewalk.

Kevin lay there stiffly, forever determined to inhabit the same moment in time. On the rough bark of the spruce, a few feet above his head, there was a mark, a smudge, a smear of red lipstick.

• FIDELITY

Bill was on his way to see Jone, his girlfriend from university days. He had flown in from Toronto yesterday, and Jennifer, his wife, was scheduled to come in tomorrow. They didn't have much time in Nova Scotia, so Bill had decided to use the extra day before Jennifer came to make the obligatory visit to an old friend.

Though he felt more comfortable with the idea of forgetting he'd ever known Jone, ceasing all contact with her forever, he was unable to carry through with it. He was obliged to make this visit, not because Jone expected it of him, but because he felt that in the eyes of his wife and of his parents, there were certain expectations of a married man. Jone and Jennifer had never met, but Bill's parents knew and liked Jone. A married man had to consider his family in his actions. A married man had to be decorous in his relationships. "Have you spoken to Jone since you've been home?" his mother might ask him one day. And what could he answer — "No, I'm afraid I may have sex with her if I see her"?

The bus smelled like Windex and cheap vinyl upholstery. The smoking section was very small, but the smoke from it had invisibly permeated the air, making the back of Bill's throat scratchy. The seats were almost all full and the heat was turned up too high. He regretted not having rented a car, but his salary at the pulp and paper company did not yet permit him that luxury.

Bill twisted his wedding band and fretted. He'd bought a copy of *Maclean's* before boarding the bus, and it sat in his lap unread. The back cover was folded back to reveal Fotheringham's column, but when he tried to read his eyes slid over the words without picking up their meaning.

Out the window, dark patches of spruce trees poked out from under a week-old crust of snow. The low grey clouds in the western sky were still lit by the sun, but over to the east, the black of night had taken root and was spreading.

"The fool has said in his heart, there is no God." Bill remembered a philosophy professor for whom that had been a favourite quotation, and the line came back to him now for the first time in more than five years. It had been on a bus ride home after Christmas exams in his second year of university, a bus ride like this one, through the dark, snow-covered woods, that his professor's words about the biblical fool had struck him to the heart. He'd been looking out the window at the snow that lay over the trees when that phrase, something he'd heard his professor say but hadn't really considered before, leapt unbidden into his heart. He'd cried then, right on the bus, short sobs escaping his throat as he tried to stifle them. The old man in the seat beside him had tried to hide behind a newspaper, but finally became so uncomfortable with Bill's crying that he got up and moved to another seat. Whether through religious insight or stress brought on by exams, tears had welled in Bill's eyes and flowed over his cheeks. I've been a fool, he'd thought in his heart. A fool. A fool. A fool.

Thinking about that now — the tears he had shed so freely in a public place, and at the prompting of a book that was thousands of years old — he wondered at his former self. He could never cry now over a few words from the Bible and some beautiful scenery. He could not even recall what that emotion, so strong as to move him to tears, had felt like. This realization saddened him. He felt bereaved, as though an important part of him had died.

He folded his *Maclean's* in two and stuffed it into the mesh pocket in front of him. Facing him was an ad for a portable stereo. The words *Choose High-Fidelity* were printed below a picture of the stereo.

Fidelity, he said to himself. He twisted the gold band at the base of his finger, slid it over the big knuckle, and let it dangle at the finger's tip. What did that word mean? He used to think it was simple. Fidelity meant he simply had to refrain from sexual contact with anyone other than his wife. But he and Jennifer had been married only six months. He had not been unfaithful, but his fidelity had not been tested.

Never in his life had he had to hold himself back sexually, especially when Jone had been his girlfriend. He and Jone had had sex whenever and wherever the whim struck either of them. They'd brought each other to climax in cars, fields, and public washrooms. They'd slipped their hands down each other's pants and masturbated each other while taking a walk down a lonely country road, stopping their walk only long enough for him to unzip his pants and ejaculate into the dust. Once, when they'd been taking the same arts elective, they'd arrived at 8:55 for a 9:15 class to find the room empty. The class scheduled for the period before had been cancelled. After fumbling around for a light switch, they'd gone in and taken their seats. Bill didn't fully remember how it had happened. He'd been taking a book from his bag when the backs of their hands touched. The next thing, they had their pants down to their ankles and were screwing like animals on the floor. They'd finished quickly, pulled their clothes back up, and were sitting quietly for almost ten minutes before another person came into the room.

When he and Jone had been together, he'd never thought of their relationship as purely sexual. They'd shared deep love and respect: honest, wholesome feelings for each other. But now that he reflected on the two years they'd been a couple, he realized that almost all of the time they'd spent together had been given over to a sexual act, its foreplay, or the quiet melancholy afterward.

To his surprise, when he tried to recall the time when he and Jone had been lovers, he found that his memories revolved around two things: his heavy schedule of studying for his Engineering classes, and their heavy schedule of sex. He remembered Philip John, the Mi'kmaq Indian from New Brunswick who sat next to him in Circuits class. He could even remember the names and faces of all his professors. But when he tried to bring to mind the colour of Jone's eyes, the sound of her voice, or simply the shape of her face, all he could recall was the smell of her naked skin, or the desperate gasp that would catch in her throat when he entered her.

Their relationship had begun at the start of their first year of university, and it had been the first sexual relationship for both of them. They became hypnotized by sex, giving themselves over to it with enthusiasm. They would meet in Bill's residence room in mornings and afternoons, whenever their free time corresponded with Bill's roommate's classes. At night they would steal time in Bill's or Jone's room while one roommate or the other was at the library or in a night class.

They were like children in their enthusiasm. They were obsessed. They tried every position they had ever heard of or could imagine. They bought pornographic magazines and read the letters from readers out loud to each other. "When they'd finished a letter, they'd do their best to duplicate the act that had been described. They became intensely concerned with orgasms, and in the back pages of one of Bill's physics notebooks, they kept track of how many they'd had. Bill had once counted more than three hundred strokes, clustered in groups of five, on the yellow sheet of graph paper, each stroke representing a final pelvic thrust, a spine curved back in ecstasy, a brief cry of pain and fear and joy.

Coming at the same time had always been their priority. But if ever Bill came first, Jone would always tell him she hadn't come yet, and he'd lie beside her and rub her until she was satisfied. Jone had always seemed more concerned with orgasms than Bill, and sometimes in Bill's room, on a weekend when his roommate had gone home, though they'd had sex three or four times that day, Jone would wake up in the middle of the night. She'd quietly switch on the radio and play it low. When Bill would wake up, the bed would be shaking ever so slightly as she rubbed herself, her moans barely concealed beneath the sound of the country and western music on the radio.

He'd lie listening to her masturbating, rising and falling along with the mattress as she quivered. Sometimes when she'd finished, he'd simply pretend he hadn't heard and drift back to sleep. Occasionally he'd roll on top of her, and they'd make love without a word, grunting and panting, then quickly dropping off after they'd both come. But several times, awakening to Jone's sighs of pleasure, he had quietly taken his penis in hand beneath the covers. Without her noticing at first, he rubbed the ridge of flesh at the edge of its head, feeling the blood rising, the tension winding within him. Gradually he increased the speed of his motions, groaning along with Jone. Without having touched each other, they'd come, the sound of the other's sighs exciting them to climax.

Bill and Jone had split up after their sophomore year, when he had had to transfer to the Technical University of Nova Scotia to continue his degree. They had not seen each other in almost five years, and apart from a phone call and a couple of letters, had had no contact in over a year.

What would happen when he saw Jone? She might be sexually aggressive, in which case he'd have to fend her off, explaining how seriously he took his wedding vows. But how could he count on himself to behave?

He was the only passenger to get off the bus in this town. The wet snow that had been falling as the bus was approaching on the highway had stopped. It had been over an hour since the sun had gone down, and the sky was completely black above the street lamps. The roads shone under melted snow.

On the main street he entered a convenience store and bought a copy of the *Chronicle-Herald*. He looked around the store for some breakfast food, bread, or cereal, but the only thing they had was a box of frosted blueberry Pop Tarts. He paid for the paper and the Pop Tarts, put them in his bag, and walked back into the night air.

A damp coolness came up from the bottom of his coat and enclosed his ribs. He wrapped his arms about himself and squeezed hard to force the chill away. He took the folded envelope from his pocket and looked at the return address in the top left corner.

He walked along the main street in front of the closed shops. The night lighting in the stores produced a shadowy, interior twilight that streaked up the walls and across the racks and shelves. He walked under the marquis of the movie house and noticed the posters in the glass doors. Even the movies listed under the Coming Soon sign had come and gone months before in Toronto.

Past a little park, the post office, and a barber shop, he found the street he was looking for and walked along it until he found the correct number. The house was a blue bungalow with two big windows facing the street. Sandwiched between the pane and curtain of each window was a small candelabra of red electric candles, a piece of tinsel garland wrapped around its base. The curtains were closed, but behind the curtains, lights glowed warmly in both windows. He rang the bell and waited. In a moment, a light came on overhead, and the wooden inside door opened. A thin, older woman appeared. She wore a powder-blue housecoat, a net over the curlers in her hair.

She peered at Bill through the aluminum storm door. She

put her face close to the glass and squinted at him. "What is it that you want?" she shouted.

"Jone," said Bill. His voice rang down the quiet street.

"What's that?" the woman said. She leaned her ear to the door until her curlers scratched against the glass.

"Jone. *Jone,*" Bill said.

The woman flipped the lock on the door and opened it. She stared at Bill intently, as though trying to memorize his features for a police artist. She pursed her lips. Little dabs of face cream clung to the corners of her mouth. After a moment of studying him, she swung her head to the side and said, "Around back."

"Around back," Bill said.

"Yes, yes," the woman said, motioning impatiently with her head.

Bill backed off her step. She leaned out the door and watched him until he had rounded the corner of the house.

The door at the back had a bare, unfrosted bulb shining over it. He rapped lightly on the glass and heard heavy footsteps on stairs. Jone had opened the door and put her arms around him before he could step inside. Her strong arms encircled him and held him in a warm, solid embrace. She smelled as she had in their university days.

"Bill, it's good to see you," she said quietly into his ear. It was dark in the little alcove inside the door. He took off his shoes and hung his coat on a peg on the wall, then followed Jone down the carpeted steps into her kitchen. He was surprised at how heavy she'd become. She was tastefully dressed in a long, loose skirt and a thick, dark angora sweater, but her hips and thighs showed round and massive beneath the folds of her skirt. Her breasts were large and firm-looking under the sweater. She'd always been on the plump side, but Bill thought she must have weighed almost double what she had the last time he'd seen her.

"Jone," he said, looking her up and down. "You look fine." In spite of the weight she'd gained, or maybe because of it, fine was the exact word for how she looked. Her weight gave her dignity, substance.

"Oh, I'm awfully fat," she said. Her face did not appear to have been touched by the extra weight, and her cheeks reddened as he looked at her.

"No," he said. "Honestly. You look . . . fine. You look . . ."

The red in her cheeks deepened. "It's really good to see you," she said finally. She motioned for him to sit at the kitchen table while she bustled about making tea.

"I brought some stuff for breakfast," Bill said. He fumbled in his bag and took out the Pop Tart box.

"Pop Tarts?" Jone said.

"I don't know," he said. "I don't want to impose."

Jone laughed. She crossed a forearm under her big bosom, as though it were difficult for her to laugh and hold up the weight of her breasts at the same time.

Bill was embarrassed by her laughter, embarrassed and a little hurt. "I don't know," he said. He brought his shoulders up and brushed his chin against his right shoulder.

"No, it's cute," Jone said. "Pop Tarts." She stopped laughing and put a hand in the middle of his back. Bill smiled at her to show he wasn't upset, and she went back to making tea.

He looked around the kitchen at the bright walls and the well-scrubbed floor. Santa in his sleigh, along with a Christmas tree and several snowmen, had been stencilled with canned snow onto the little window over the sink. A string of minilights blinked on and off around the window's perimeter. An array of Christmas cards was stuck to the fridge with coloured magnets. He recognized a card that was from him and Jennifer.

"This looks like a good place," he said.

"It's not bad for now," she said. "The rent is cheap. I'll show you the rest after we've had tea."

"I met your landlady," Bill said, he couldn't help smirking.

"Oh, that old —" she stopped herself. "Don't let her bother you. The poor soul doesn't have a friend in the world. She deliberately scares people off. She's not so bad."

"She's got a lovely set of curlers," Bill said. "I'll say that much for her."

Jone set the kettle on the burner to boil, placed a tin of homemade muffins on the table, and sat down across from Bill. They chuckled together about the landlady's curlers. Jone leaned her head to one side as she laughed and showed her large teeth.

"How is Jennifer?" Jone asked.

It was strange to hear Jone say Jennifer's name. The two women had never met, and though he'd told Jennifer most of what there was to know about Jone, Jone knew almost nothing about Jennifer.

"She's fine," Bill said. "She's still in Toronto. She'll be flying out tomorrow afternoon. She said to tell you she's sorry she can't meet you this time. We only have a few days, and we want to spend them with Mum and Dad. They only met Jen once, and it was a pretty busy time with the wedding and all. You two will meet next time."

"It's too bad," Jone said. She held her hands out to him. "Show me your ring."

Bill gave her his hand, and she pulled it toward her. "It's only a band," he said. "Just a plain, gold band." Her fingers were short, with dimples at the knuckles. She held his hand firmly as she looked at the ring.

"That's the best kind," she said, examining the ring intently. "It's a nice symbol. A wedding band." She released his hand and sat back in her chair. They smiled at each other across the table as the sound of steam rose in the kettle, then died away.

They talked for a time about friends from University days, shared some gossip about who was getting married and who was living where. Now and then over his tea, or when he leaned across the table to pick up another muffin, he got a sniff of Jone's perfume. It was a girl's scent, and seemed out of place on this large, solid woman across from him. The memories Jone's smell aroused put him off, and he soon found his shoulders tensely squared.

When the teapot was empty, Jone stood up, smoothed her skirt and sweater, and said, "Let me show you the place." Bill took his bag and followed her into the living room. As they passed out of the kitchen, she pointed to a door on the left. "That's the bathroom," she said. She switched on a light in the living room. The carpet was clean, but it was old and worn. The furniture was the same. The couch sagged in the middle, and the coffee table had a long scratch across the top. In contrast, a brand new TV stood on a low table in the corner. On top of the TV stood a small artificial tree, lushly decorated, its lights glowing in blue and red and green. On the wall above the tree hung a poster print of a couple kissing that Bill recognized from Jones residence room.

At the end of the couch was a pile of bedding with a pillow on top. "Here's where you'll sleep," Jone said definitely, as though to dispel any questions. Near the foot of the couch was her bedroom door. She switched on her bedroom light and Bill looked inside. The room was barely large enough for the single bed it held. The bed was neatly made and piled high with thick blankets and quilts. There was a small bookshelf on the wall over the bed. A tiny dresser, cluttered with a woman's things, stood in a corner. On the dresser was a small, square clock radio.

They sat awhile in the living room and talked, but there were too many topics, all related to the past, that Bill tried to steer the conversation away from. They soon fell silent. Bill pulled absently at the pills on the fabric of the couch. He excused himself and went into the bathroom. In the mirror over the little sink he saw his flushed cheeks. When he lifted the toilet seat and unzipped his fly, he was surprised to find a long, sore erection tucked down the leg of his pants. He had to splash it with cold water from the sink before he could pee. After he'd finished, he washed his hands and splashed cold water on his face.

When he got back to the living room he clapped his hands together and said, "Well, what do you do for excitement in this town?"

Jone laughed and said, "I've been asking myself that question since the day I arrived."

"Is there a decent bar?" he asked.

"There's a bar, but it's not decent," she said.

Bill marched about the room, circling the chair Jone sat in, hemming comically about what they should do. "I know," he said finally. "When do the movies show?"

They walked along the street bundled in their thick clothes. Blinking Christmas lights outlined the wood-framed houses. Lavishly decorated trees stood ostentatiously before picture windows whose curtains were drawn back. Now and again Jone would point out the house of another teacher at her school, or of a favourite student, or of somebody famous in the town — a doctor, or the mayor, or the family who owned the grocery store. When they arrived at the cinema, they each paid for their own ticket.

The woman at the ticket window had her hair dyed an unnatural shade of brown. A crescent of metallic blue eye shadow hung heavily over each eye. "Hello there," the woman said to Jone. This was a way, Bill thought, to let Jone know that the woman knew who she was. As Bill handed the money for his ticket through the space in the window, the woman caught sight of his wedding ring.

"Hmm," Bill heard her say. She raised her eyebrows and stretched her upper lip down in a frown. Bill waited for her to say something, but she merely gave him his change.

It was early. The first show wasn't yet half finished. They bought a small popcorn and sat on a padded bench in the lobby. The woman at the ticket window craned her neck shamelessly around her cash register to watch them.

"What's it like?" Jone said. "Being married."

Bill was startled. What a question! "It's like . . ." He paused, looking up at the ceiling of the lobby, trying to avoid eye contact with the cashier. "It's like not being married," he said. "Except . . ." He paused again, then shook his head.

"I always thought we'd get married," Jone said.

Bill felt his insides tighten.

"You and me, I mean. Even after we broke up. Even when we hadn't spoken a word in months. I don't know what I was thinking. Maybe fate or something. I still feel sad."

Emotion welled up in him. Tears pushed to get out of his eyes.

He looked up at the woman at the cash register, who

appeared intrigued and surprised to see his eyes glistening. He stood up. "Why don't you show me a bit of the town?" he said.

They left the cinema and walked back up the main street, passed the turn for Jone's house, and continued to a place near the edge of town, where the houses got farther and farther apart. The streetlights came to an end, and they were walking on a dirt road. The sky had cleared, and beneath the light of stars, fields of dry corn stalks stuck out of frozen snow on both sides of the road. Where the rows of corn ended, the black woods began.

After a wide bend in the road, they came to a big steel-frame bridge whose beams rose above them and sliced across the sky. They stopped in the middle of the bridge and leaned against the chest-high rail. The sound of the river rushing over rocks, and the cold, clean smell of the water rose up to them.

"What do you think I'm going to do now?" Bill said. He looked at Jone and smiled. She looked at him seriously for a moment, then smiled and said, "You're going to spit."

Bill brought some saliva to the front of his mouth and spat it down into the river. They both laughed. A cold wind blew down the river and through their clothing.

Bill remembered how they had once known every bump, fold, and blemish of the other's skin. They had lain in each other's arms until late in the night, dreaming out loud about a future they thought they would spend together. What they had shared had been real, Bill thought now. In some way, their dreams were still real. They had loved each other. They'd been too important to each other for their feelings to ever disappear completely. Standing now so far apart, they were acting two sad roles in a sad play. They were pretending the past had never happened. They were pretending they didn't know each other any more.

Bill thought longingly of Jennifer and the tenderness he felt for her, the fidelity he owed her. That was love, he thought. But he loved Jone, too, though it was a different love. His love for Jone was the deep tenderness owed to one human being from another to whom she has bared her heart. The water below them rushed past in the dark. Snow on the banks caught in the swirling ripples and was carried away. Here and there a dark lump of ice jutted above the water's surface, turned slowly about, then drifted out of sight below the bridge. Without a word, Bill moved in close to Jone and put his arm about her shoulders.

They were a few minutes late for the second show. The usher tore their tickets in silence and waved them into the lobby. The woman at the cash register eyed them steadily as they crossed the lobby and went into the theatre. The place was almost empty. They passed a middle-aged couple at the back of the theatre and an old man by himself farther on. Down in front sat a row of six or seven teenagers. Bill and Jone took seats about halfway back from the screen, took off their coats, and hung them over the seats in front of them.

The movie was not very engaging. It was a big-budget Hollywood production about a group of middle-class college graduates in New York. As the movie progressed, he began to think about having put his arm around Jone on the bridge. He knew in his heart that he had touched her out of a feeling of deep friendship and affection, but he began to wonder about how she had interpreted his action. They hadn't talked about it, and he'd taken his arm away from her before they had walked back into town. Did she know that there had only been friendship in that embrace? Did she realize that he had no intention of betraying Jennifer? He recalled now a discussion he and Jone had once had about the idea of fidelity. It had been in their second year at university, when Bill was taking Philosophy 100 as his arts elective. Being exposed to so many different and conflicting ideas in the survey course had shaken his whole world view. He'd abandoned every idea of morality he'd ever had, and for a time, having recognized social norms as arbitrary, he'd rejected them for pretending to be otherwise. "I'm not saying that faithfulness to a single sexual partner is a bad idea," he recalled himself saying. "I just don't see why it should be the only moral idea." He suddenly felt he'd made a terrible mistake back on the bridge. He took his arm from the armrest between them and brought it close to his side.

There wasn't much to say about the picture when it ended. They put on their coats in silence and walked back to Jone's. Twice on the way home, Bill felt Jone move a little closer to him as they walked, and both times he withdrew.

They were awkward with each other when they got to Jone's place. Jone turned on the TV, and they watched the end of the late news. They were both chilled from the cold walk to the river, the warm theatre, followed by the cold walk home. Bill put his arms about his sides and felt the chill deepen as he hugged himself. Jone warmed them each a cup of milk. "I'm going to get a hot shower," she said when she'd drained her cup. Bill heard her moving about in her bedroom for a few moments, then, in a housecoat and slippers, she stepped from her bedroom into the bathroom.

While she showered, he found himself imagining her body, wet beneath the spray. He shook his head and covered his ears with his hands to shut out the sound of the shower, but he couldn't stop thinking of her in there, rubbing soapy hands over her skin. Her face glowed when she came from the bathroom. She had a towel wrapped turban-style around her hair. The housecoat was pulled tightly about her, and the smell of scented talc filled the room.

"I feel much better," she said. "You should have a shower. It'll warm you up."

"I feel a lot warmer now," Bill said. He wanted to go into the bathroom just to get away from her, but he was afraid to stand up. He was sure Jone would notice his erection.

She sat in the armchair opposite him, and leaning slightly forward, unwrapped, then re-wrapped the towel on her hair. Bill felt his throat tighten as he looked through the front of her housecoat and saw the line of cleavage where her full breasts came together. When she looked up, she saw him gazing at her breasts. For a moment their eyes met in passion and embarrassment. Her nipples rose against the fabric of her robe.

"So what do you think of the town?" Jone said suddenly, standing up from her chair. "It must seem pretty boring compared with Toronto."

"Toronto. Toronto. Toronto," Bill said. He tried to swallow, but his throat was too dry. "Toronto's not all you think it is before you go there." He breathed deeply through his nose.

"I hope you can stay for lunch tomorrow," she said. "There's a lovely little sandwich shop off the main street. I'd like to treat you."

"I think I should take off first thing," he said. "I have to take Dad's car and drive to the airport. Jennifer's plane comes in at two."

"I see," she said. "I'll fix us a nice breakfast then, before you go." She walked slowly to her bedroom door, then turned and said: "I don't suppose . . ." Her eyes met his for a moment, then shifted away.

Bill's mouth went dry again.

"I think I'll hit the hay," Jone said at last. "You can still take a shower if you like."

Bill forced air through his thick throat. "Thanks," he said.

She entered her bedroom and closed the door behind her.

He slumped against the back of the couch and put his hands to his face. He shook his head. This is craziness, he thought. Craziness.

He spread the blankets and sheets across the couch, took off his sweater, pants, and socks, and after shutting off the light, climbed under the sheets in his T-shirt and boxers. His eyes slowly adjusted to the dark. He looked about the strange room and knew he'd awaken in the morning and have no idea where he was. On the other side of the wall, the bedsprings creaked as Jone got into bed. She tossed about several times before settling in.

He snapped on the lamp at the head of the couch and blinked in the light that flooded the room. He reached around on the floor until he found his overnight bag. He took out the copy of the *Chronicle-Herald* he'd bought and glanced at the front page. The news had not changed since he was in high school. Petty political scandals and a slowly bleeding economy. He flipped through the pages in search of the national weather. It was minus four degrees and cloudy in Toronto. He imagined the view from his apartment window, the little tree-lined playground across the street. Jennifer might just be closing the curtains on that scene now, before going to bed. He folded the paper twice and placed it on the floor, then reached up and switched off the light.

He had almost drifted off to sleep when a radio snapped on. Muted country and western music came through the wall from Jone's bedroom. Quietly at first, almost lost in the sound of the radio, then growing gradually more audible, he heard the little squeaks of her bedsprings shaking.

A rush of heat passed over his throat and down his chest. It moved across the skin of his belly, raising the hairs there as it moved. As the rhythm of the bedsprings continued, he put a hand under his T-shirt and passed it over his chest. A spark of electricity jumped through him as he touched a stiff nipple. He lowered his hand along his warm belly. He took his hard penis in his palm and squeezed it until it hurt. He closed his eyes tight and tried to form a picture of Jennifer. He thought of the last time they'd made love, the night before he'd left Toronto. He imagined Jennifer's lips on his skin. He pictured her small, round breasts, her smooth, white thighs.

Jone rolled over, bouncing heavily on the bed and letting out a soft moan. She bumped the wall, sending a jolt through the couch on which Bill lay. What the hell, he thought. He opened his eyes and moved his thoughts to Jone's round, warm body on the bed in the next room. He carefully formed a picture of her stout breasts, her wide hips. He imagined his hands moving over her smooth skin. He formed an O with his lips and pretended they were encircling a nipple.

Jone moaned again, as though in response to his thoughts.

"Yes," he whispered into the dark room as he squeezed his erection harder. He sat up and pressed an ear to the wall, trying to detect a noise above the music on the radio. The bed creaked, high and tinny. Faintly through the music, he thought he heard a low throaty sound.

• A NEW START

It's just before dark, and I look through the crack in the blind to the street. Mum passes in front of the liquor store. The Salvation Army man sits propped against the store's black, polished-stone front. His chair is so close to its own reflection in the stone that it looks like there are two chairs and two Salvation Army men: one pair growing out of the other's back. He holds his tambourine out to Mum as she goes by, but she's got her back to that place. She don't see him. Mum doesn't like that our new apartment is so close to the liquor store.

"You call this a new start," she said to Daddy. "I know what kind of start it'll be."

Daddy said, "It's what we can afford right now."

Mum said, "I don't like it, the liquor store."

Daddy said, "It's what we can afford."

Mum comes in after all day. She's got two boxes of Kraft Dinner in a Sobey's bag. She puts the bag on the table and goes, "That's it, Jim."

Daddy goes, "That's it."

Mum takes a nickel and a penny from her pocket and puts them on the counter. "That's it," she goes. Daddy don't say nothing but he walks into the bathroom and he don't come out for a while.

"Kids gotta have something warm to eat," Mum goes.

There's this big crash from the bathroom. Mum tells me and Beth to go to our room. Beth goes, "We ain't got no room."

Mum goes, "Shut up." So me and Beth lie down on the pull-out couch we sleep on.

The bathroom door opens and Mum goes stiff. She looks at Daddy and goes, "Kids gotta have something warm to eat."

"This is a new start," Daddy goes. "I said this was gonna be a new start, and I meant it." He takes the broom and dust pan and sweeps up the pieces of the mirror.

I remember the look on his face when we moved in here. His chest got all big and he sniffed in the dusty air. "A new start," he said, all smiling and happy. He put Beth up on his shoulders and danced around the empty room.

Almost a month and this room is still empty.

After we eat the Kraft Dinner, Mum lies down on the couch. She pulls her feet up into her hands and starts to rub them.

"These poor old dogs," she goes. "Me poor old dogs."

Daddy sits at the end of the couch and rubs her feet for

a while. Even after she falls asleep, he keeps rubbing them. "Poor old dogs," he goes.

Now it's our turn. We go out at night so the Child Welfare don't see. They don't know we're in town yet. Daddy don't want them to know. Not till we save up enough money for some new clothes. Daddy says we got to make a good impression, what with school on. Him and Mum have been sober for a while now, and we need some new clothes and a few sticks of furniture. That'll be a start, Daddy says.

We begin each night at the mall. There's a big dumper behind the Met. Once we found this pair of stretchy jeans in it that were only a little too big for Beth. You never know what people will throw out, not to mention bottles. There's a Sobey's at the mall too, with two big, smelly dumpers. We never root there, though. We're not pigs yet, Daddy says. We're not pigs yet to be eating throwed-away food.

Tonight is not too cold for September. You can only see your breath a little. At the back of the mall there are these lights that make big triangles on the wall. We can see the Met dumper at the other end. It's the biggest dumper and it's got the biggest triangle over it. All the way along there are smaller dumpers and just plain cans.

Daddy has a broken hockey stick, and he pokes it into the cans as we walk. One swish around the outside and a swipe through the middle and you can pretty well tell if there's any good bottles. Bottles you can't take back go clunk or clank when you hit them. They're big, useless plastic pop bottles and the little ones with Styrofoam around them. The good bottles are the dark brown beer bottles or the big, swirly Pepsi bottles. They hoot. Just like an owl. *Hoot!* They're practically sending you messages, waiting to be rescued.

Daddy stops under a light and blows breath-smoke up at the sky. He leans on his hockey stick, takes a puff or two of his fingers, and blows up another cloud.

"I do fancy a cigarette," he goes. He talks in an English accent. Beth and me laugh. Daddy swings his stick back and forth and walks like Charlie Chaplin. "Jolly old chap," he goes.

As we come up to the first can, Daddy runs ahead of me and Beth. He stops, takes the lid off the can, and goes, "Hoot. Hoot," down into the can. That's good luck, he says. It's the lucky bottle call. He sticks his stick in and swishes it around. Clank, clunk. Nothing.

He does a funny run to the next can, and Beth and me laugh. "Hoot. Hoot." Nothing there either. He slams the lid down.

We go like this right to the Met dumper, only by the time we get there, Daddy's not doing his lucky bottle call no more. He don't run ahead neither. Me and Beth get there before him. We wait, and he gives us each a boost up into the dumper. This you got to dig through. There's just too much. It's mostly paper tonight, paper and cardboard. I dig in one corner, Beth digs in another. Daddy is the look-out.

"There ain't nothing in here, Daddy," Beth goes. "Just papers."

"Keep looking," Daddy goes.

"But, Daddy, there ain't nothing." Beth is right. Big, useless boxes, plastic bags, and paper.

"Just make sure," Daddy goes.

Beth and me root and root. We squat down, dig our hands in deep, and pull up paper between our feet. We work side by side and then back to back. I push stuff up from the bottom, then Beth digs through it. There's nothing in here.

Daddy sticks his head up over the edge of the dumper and goes, "Get down."

"There's nothing," I go.

"Get down and stay down," he goes, his voice all tight. The whole back wall of the mall goes lit up with headlights. Daddy climbs up the side of the dumper and makes like he's rooting.

"I'm scared," Beth goes.

Through his teeth Daddy whispers, "Don't be scared. Cops." He makes like he's swishing some paper around. The car pulls up to the dumper. Daddy goes into his drunk act.

Cop Voice goes, "Hey you! What you doing there?"

"I'm just a drunk, officer," Daddy goes. "Just a drunk. I ain't hurting nobody."

"Well, Mr. Drunk," Cop Voice goes. "You get the hell outta here. You here me? This ain't no soup kitchen. This here's private property."

Me and Beth are crouched down, trying not to breathe. We don't know which would be worse, the cops taking us away again, or the noises Daddy makes when they take us. Daddy jumps down. We hear him stagger away. Scuff. Scuff.

The cop car don't move. Beth starts almost crying, quiet. We hear a cop radio. One of the cops gets out of the car. His cop shoes click-click on the ground. *He knows we're in here. He knows we're in here.* Then the lid bangs shut. The lights go out. The cop car drives away.

When Daddy comes back and opens the lid, Beth is crying out loud. I jump down out of the can. Daddy lifts Beth out and holds her. She keeps crying.

"Don't you worry about them cops, Bethy," Daddy goes. "Goddam cops."

We go to the university next. We cross a big field to get there. Halfway across the field you can see all the lights lit up on the campus. Everybody has their own little room.

Usually we already have something by the time we get to the university. This time alls we got's the empty Sobey's bags we stuffed in our pockets before we come out. Daddy's pretty quiet. He carries Beth piggy-back.

You never know where you might find bottles here. You have to check all the garbage cans. Mostly the odd beer bottle is what you get, but they add up. Once in a while you come on a whole stack. Three or four or five empty flats.

Most of the lights are on in the first big building, even though it's late. You can see some TVs going. Daddy gets me and Beth to do the cans by the door. I get one from my can, Beth gets three from hers. Daddy goes down into the courtyard by himself. Me and Beth stand and watch.

First he goes back and forth across the lawn. We see some windows open, some faces. Daddy stops and puts a bottle in his bag.

"Hey, what you looking for?" a voice goes. "You looking for bottles?" Hoot! A bottle comes down and hits the lawn. Daddy don't look to where it come from. He runs over and picks it up.

"Hey, you guys! This guy wants bottles! Can we help him out?" Hoot! Hoot! Two more bottles come down. Daddy jumps back from where they hit. He bends over and puts them in his bag.

Now there is a face in most every window. Bottles hoot and hoot. Some of them break. Daddy stops putting them in his bag and just piles them in a pile. He jumps back when one almost hits him. It rains bottles. The faces in the windows laugh and holler. "Hey, bottle man. Let's see you dance for a bottle." One wings down and almost hits Daddy's feet till he jumps out of the way.

Beth tries to run down to Daddy, but I hold her back. "Daddy!" she goes.

Daddy turns his sour face over his shoulder. "Piss on them," he says.

It's a long time till they get tired of throwing bottles. Daddy never gets tired of picking them up. When we leave, all the windows in the building are closed up again, most of the lights are off. Every bag we come with is full.

Daddy waves me and Beth down to help carry. "Boy, Daddy," I go. "We don't have to go nowheres else tonight." He don't smile at me. He don't say nothing. I smell the sour smell of beer.

On the way to the Quik Pik store, we stop and sit in the seats by the football field.

Beth goes, "I don't wanna stop. I wanna go home. I wanna go to bed."

Daddy goes, "Wait a minute."

Beth goes, "Can't we go home now? Can't we just sell them and go home? I'm cold."

Daddy takes off his coat and puts it around her. "Just you wait a bit, Bethy," he goes.

He starts taking the bottles out of the bags. Beth lies down on a bench. She slept all day, but it's getting late. It's getting to be early in the morning. She conks right out. Daddy takes each bottle, and one by one he pours the little beer drops from them into one bottle. I lie down beside Beth.

I wake up when I hear Daddy sigh. He sits back. He holds the beer bottle up to the light. It's not quite full. I watch him tip it back and down it in one drink. He smacks his lips. He looks down at me and sees I'm awake.

"Just a taste," he goes.

"I never said nothing," I go.

Back home Mum is still asleep on the couch. It's just getting light outside.

"Where am I going to sleep now?" Beth goes.

Daddy goes, "Shh," not to wake Mum. He sets the money we made on the counter. He puts a blanket on the floor for Beth and me. We curl up together and he puts his winter coat over us. Beth goes right to sleep.

I lie there with one eye half open. Daddy sits scrunched in the corner, his knees up. He looks up to where the money is. I can hear him breathe in deep, breathe out his nose. He looks over at Mum asleep. Breathe in. Looks at me and Beth. I close my eye. Breathe out.

When the floor creaks, I open my eyes again. Daddy walks across to the money. He crumples up the bills, puts them in his pocket, and goes out the door.

I get up and peek out the crack in the blind. The sun is up. There is Daddy, sitting on the sidewalk and leaning against the black, polished-stone front of the liquor store. It's not open yet. Daddy's reflection makes it look like there are two of him. One in daylight, one in night. One facing our new apartment, one turned away.

"Look," you said. "It's not the oil. You know damn well."

The tank was dry, the furnace out, the house cold.

"You just said it was," I said. Anger rose inside me. "Didn't you just say it was the oil?"

"I said the oil was one more thing. It's not the oil. The oil was an example."

We sat across the kitchen table from each other. Late fall sunlight came thin and narrow into the room, surrounding us in a bright, desolate glow. Despite the light it brought, the sun was unable to warm us in our house, and we spoke in the tense voices of people who have hardened themselves against the cold.

"I wish you'd make up your mind," I said. "Is it the oil, or isn't it? It can't be the oil and not the oil. It can't be both."

You opened your mouth as if to say something, then closed your mouth and lowered your head. You frowned and shook your head slowly.

"What?" I said. "What? You were going to say something. Say it."

You shook your head again, then took a drink of your coffee, slurping it over the rim of your cup. You held the coffee in your mouth an instant, then swallowed it.

I picked my feet from the floor. My skates were laced on snugly, and despite the bulky plastic blade guards, felt nimble. I sighed and let the skates drop to the floor, to punctuate my sigh.

Hortense, the cat, leapt to my lap. I brought my hands to her sides, but before I could hold her, she jumped to the table. "Hey," I said, but I didn't have the energy to shoo her down. You looked at Hortense distractedly. You reached to the table and picked up your coffee, took a drink. Your gaze passed through Hortense and through the table. You turned your head, and your gaze passed through me, through the wall behind me, and out into the world beyond our house. Hortense began to lap at some milk that lay in the bottom of a bowl with a few soggy Rice Krispies.

"You're not leaving me," I said. I looked at you, expecting you to laugh. Your eyes focused on me, zeroed in, and pushed against me.

You rose from your chair and lifted Hortense from the table. She made no complaint, and when you put her on the floor, she walked slowly and coolly into the living room. You looked so different without skates on, so short. Your feet looked small and delicate. The lines of reinforced nylon across the ends of your stockings darkened your toes, but apart from these, your feet appeared white and vulnerable against the black blade guard marks that scarred the tiles.

From the fridge you removed the milk, opened a corner of the carton, and sniffed at the opening. You took a spoon from the table, rinsed it under the tap, and smoothed milk into my coffee. You topped your own cup with coffee from the pot.

"I don't know," you said. You sat back down at the table. I waited a moment for you to continue, but you said nothing.

"You don't know," I said. "What don't you know?" Some emotion appeared in your eyes. You sucked both lips into your mouth and bit down on them, letting them roll out of your mouth as you bit down. Your body tensed, then went limp. You let out a moan.

"I'm tired," you said. "Tired, tired, tired." This was something you'd said before, but I looked at you now, and you *looked* tired. You looked tired down through your flesh.

"Tired of everything," you said. "Tired of me. Tired of you. Tired of us." You pressed your thumbs into your temples and made circles. "I feel like putting a bullet in my head," you said. You closed your eyes and pressed a palm to your forehead, wincing as though a lead slug were passing through your skull.

"Jesus. I'm tired of saying I'm tired," you said.

"Honey," I said. "Why don't we talk about this?"

You jumped from your seat, knocking over your coffee.

"I'm tired of talking!" you screamed. You started to laugh. You bent over, put your hands on your knees, and laughed so hard I thought you would vomit.

I began laughing, too. At first my laughter came only from my throat, but soon my stomach ached with the bellows that came from me. I clutched at my stomach and slid off my chair to the floor. I fell onto my back and bumped my head. It hurt like hell, but that only made me laugh harder, and I could see it had the same effect on you.

Struggling for breath, you ran the sleeves of your blouse over your eyes to wipe back the tears. I thought my stomach would burst, it was so tight.

"Honey!" I called to you between guffaws. "Honey!"

I rolled onto my stomach and struggled to my knees. I pulled a hand away from my sore belly and held it out to you. With my arm extended, I crawled in your direction. "Honey," I said.

Fighting laughter, you straightened up, wiped the tears from your cheeks, and smoothed your skirt over your legs. You looked down at me with more emotion than I'd seen on your face all morning.

"Fuck it!" you said. You were still laughing as you turned and walked out of the kitchen.

"Honey! Honey!" I called after you. I stood up with some difficulty, my laughter getting in the way. I followed you through the living room and into the front entrance. "What's going on?" I said. You opened the door to the front porch, and the cold came rushing in. "What are you doing?" I said.

You stood on the bare porch floor and began putting on your tall, fleece-lined boots. Without your skates on, you barely came up to the middle of my chest. You didn't look at me; you were concentrating on zipping a boot up your calf. A tear of laughter came to your eye, and you wiped it away with your wrist.

"Am I crazy, or does none of this make sense?" I said.

You took your quilted coat from the chrome coat rack. As you put it on, I noticed the suitcase that had been hidden in the long folds of the coat.

"What's this?" I said, pointing at the suitcase.

"My suitcase," you said.

"I know it's your suitcase," I said.

When you had the coat buttoned, you picked up the suitcase and looked at me for a moment. You looked serious now.

"You're not leaving me," I said. My head felt strange, as though there were a hole through the top of it, and everything from inside were escaping. I put my hands over the top of my head and pushed down to keep what I could from spilling out.

You opened the suitcase, revealing what was inside: your skates. I felt my mouth open. "What can you possibly be thinking of?" I said. In reply, you grasped the knot where the laces were tied together and lifted the skates from the case. Holding them at arm's length, you let them drop to the floor with a thump. You closed the empty suitcase and tucked it under your arm. Without a word, you turned and walked out the door.

I panicked and ran to the door after you. I stood on the wooden landing of the step with my mouth open. "You're not leaving me!" I shouted.

You stopped on the sidewalk and turned around to look at me. I waited for you to say something, but when you didn't, I raised my hands from my sides. I was asking you to explain.

"Goodbye," you said. There was no malice on your face. You wore an expression of peace. You turned and walked down the sidewalk.

I stayed on the front step until you'd disappeared from sight. A small square of the front yard lay in the shadow of the house, but soon the sun would be in the western half of the sky, beginning its descent from day into night, and even the narrow strip of shadow that now remained on the lawn would be gone.

The grass of the front lawn was dry and brown; the last tinge of green had left it. There was a trace of frost on the tips of the grass blades closest to the house. On the concrete blocks of the front walk, there were patches of shell ice in the places where the lowest corner of one block met the highest corner of the one beside it. Each thin, translucent sheet of ice was broken by a web of fissures, where your foot had gone through.

My skates clunked loudly against the wooden steps as I descended to the walk. I crouched over the closest ice patch to get a good look. Delicate, triangular shards lay on the frosty concrete. In the spot where your heel had gone through, the ice was crushed to dust.

I called the oil company about the furnace. The man who answered was sympathetic, but he wanted me to understand that this was the first cold spell of the season, and the orders for oil were backed up.

"I'm going to freeze here," I said. "The tank is dry."

"We'll put you on the Priority List," the man said. His voice was deep and authoritative, and what he said about a Priority List reassured me. "We've been run ragged here today," the man continued. "We'll be going around the clock. I'm the dispatcher, but after four I'll be going out in a delivery truck myself. That's the situation we have here now." He paused and gave a sigh of exasperation. When he uttered his next word, however, his voice had regained its tone of positive authority.

"People don't prepare," he said. "They know winter is coming, but they act as if summer lasts all year long.

Everything is last minute. We'll get to you. It may be early tomorrow morning before we do, but —"

"Early tomorrow morning!" I said.

"Two, three, four o'clock," the oil man said.

"What am I supposed to do until then!" I wanted to know.

"Dress warmly," he said. "Especially your head. So few people realize the importance of a warm head. You should cover your feet, too, of course." I looked down at my big warm skates and smiled. "But eighty percent of your body's heat loss goes right out the top of your head. The head is a chimney," the oil man said. "It's the body's chimney, so keep that chimney covered."

Following the advice of the oil man, I went to the bedroom and dressed warmly. First, I took off my skates and put on my one-piece long underwear and flannel pyjamas. I stretched my hockey socks up my legs and fastened them to my pyjama pants with safety pins. I sat down on the bed and picked up one of my skates from the floor. I examined it in the light that came through the window. The side panels were made of black nylon mesh. The toe cap was covered with mesh. The main seam on each side and the support at the heel were made from brown leather. The blades were stainless steel Tuuk blades, and I remembered that when I'd bought the skates, Tuuk blades were new. Mine must have been one of the first pairs of CCM Tacks to use Tuuks. The salesman had advised me against them, I remembered. He'd recommended the regular steel tubing.

"To tell you the truth, I don't trust these things," he'd said. "They look flimsy. Listen to this." He flicked a finger against the plastic tubing and shook his head at the ticking sound.

I stood up from the bed and took a step forward. My bare

heels and toes protruded from the hockey socks and felt odd on the carpet. My feet were so weak and insignificant without skates. I stood before the mirror that hung on the back of the bedroom door and noticed how, without skates, I looked not only shorter, but thinner. Being able to wiggle my toes freely was good for a change, but I felt wobbly on my feet. I walked to the closet and opened the door. There was a chest of drawers inside and I slid the bottom drawer open. In the drawer there were dozens of pairs of shoes. Some were dusty and as many as ten years old. Some were shiny and new. But there was not a scuff mark in the entire drawer. Every pair, old and new, had a sole that had never come in contact with the ground. I looked out the bedroom window in time to see a big Ford station wagon slowly making its way down the street.

I wonder what it would be like, I thoughr. Then I realized that it was too late. I closed the drawer and sat back down on the bed. I put on my skates and laced them up again. I ran my fingers through my hair and thought about my tuque. The head is a chimney, the oil man had said.

I stomped down the stairs and into the front porch, where I found my tuque stuffed into a sleeve of my down-filled coat. Like two amputated feet, your skates lay on the dark floor. A chill went through me at the thought of the word: amputated. I remembered a story I'd read at school. The story involved a disembodied monkeys paw, dry and shrivelled, that had come into the household of a poor and hapless family.

What I recalled about the story was the tragic death of the family's son as a result of a wish they'd made on the monkey's paw, supposedly a lucky talisman. The family then wished their son would come back. And one night he did return. His ghoulish body escaped the grave and came pounding at the door. Their son had become a zombie: one of the living dead.

I bent down and picked your skates from the floor, my heart racing in my chest. Out the front door I tossed them, out onto the lawn. I shut the door quickly and hooked the latch before the skates could get back in. I shuddered.

I took my grey tuque from the sleeve of the down-filled coat and pulled it over my ears. Wearing a tuque indoors felt ridiculous. I was desperate, following the orders of an oil man I had never met. But with the tuque on I was warmer, safer somehow. I felt protected from whatever evil might lie inside or outside the house. I donned the coat and pulled on the mitts that were in its pockets. My hands felt thick and powerful in mitts, and I jauntily slapped the leather palms together.

The sun had passed into the western sky, and the light that landed in the kitchen was in narrow strips on the floor near the north wall. I took a ceramic beer mug from the cupboard and poured the remaining coffee into it. The milk was still on the table where you'd left it. I picked it up, sniffed at the open spout, and poured some into my mug.

I studied the cups and bowls left from breakfast. The chair you'd been sitting in stood at an odd angle — where it had landed when you leapt to your feet. A drool of coffee leaked through the seam in the centre of the tabletop, collecting in a puddle on the floor. Out of curiosity, I took off one of my mitts and crouched to touch the spilled coffee. It was as cold as the rest of the room.

I went into the living room and sat in front of the TV. In the dead screen my own reflection sat slumped against the vinyl couch, raising and lowering the mug of coffee.

Hortense wandered languidly about the house. She went upstairs, and as the afternoon wore on, I heard her walking from one room to another, following the movement of the sun from window to window. When the sun had finally gone, she bumped down the stairs and curled into my lap for warmth.

For most of the evening I sat before the TV, my legs wrapped in a quilt, toe caps of my skates poking up beyond the quilt's end. I held the remote in my hand and nipped from channel to channel, looking for something that would hold my attention. By the time the CBC late movie came on, my head was pounding. I felt weak in the arms and legs, and there was a painful emptiness in my stomach. It occurred to me that I had not eaten a thing all day. I had drunk that coffee in the morning, and that had been it.

I stood up, my legs wobbling beneath me. My feet were pins and needles. My head swam. I stamped my skates into the floor until some of the feeling came back to my feet, then I went into the kitchen. I turned on the light and blinked in the glare until my pupils adjusted.

The curtains on the window gaped open, revealing a black pane. The faint scent of the morning's coffee mixed with the smell of dirty dishes. The bag of bread on the counter was open, and when I reached into it, the first two slices were dry and hard. I stuffed a corner of the third piece into my mouth. Turning my back on the kitchen, I snapped off the light. I tore off a piece of bread with my teeth and chewed on it as I crossed the living room. I shut off the TV on my way through.

The house was completely dark now, except for the dim light that crept in from outside. I finished eating the bread as I climbed the stairs, and it settled to my stomach in a lump. In the bathroom I brushed my teeth and laughed out loud at the sight of myself bundled in a coat, hat, and mitts in my own house.

I shut off the bathroom light and felt my way along the wall in the hallway. I opened the bedroom door and fell into bed, exhausted. There was a loud meowing as Hortense leapt from the bed to the floor. I pulled the tuque down snugly over my ears, drew the blankets up over my face, and fell immediately to sleep.

Soon came the skating.

The lake was a plate of polished ice — frozen evenly, completely free of snow.

The cold air filled my lungs, and my breath sent steam up in front of my face as I charged up the lake. White of shaved ice rose from the edges where my blades cut in.

The ice spread before me, getting longer, not shorter, as I raced to the faraway end of it. The trees and rocks on both sides of the lake looked small and grey and dry on shore. Above them on both sides and following the shoreline in either direction were two roads: a gravel road on the west side of the lake, a paved road on the east. The sky was clear and blue, and reflected in a bluish hue off the white, white snow that rose above the roads to cover the steep hills on either side of the lake. Columns of whitish, brownish wood smoke rose thin and straight as pencils from the chimneys of houses on the hills.

Now and then as I skated, my blades bumped a narrow, black crevice. Occasionally, over the sound of my blades cutting the surface, came the massive groaning of the ice, the rubbing of one huge ice sheet against another.

The lake narrowed, and I swerved out to stay clear of a

finger of land. Beyond this finger, the lake widened again, and I found myself in a loop of indented shore. Near a small cluster of trees, dark outlines wavered on the bright ice. People skating. As I drew closer I could make out a woman and three children. They were dressed well for winter weather and were skating in small, careful circles near the shore.

Without warning, a loud and intrusive noise cut through the air. A car horn. I looked at the road and saw a dark vehicle come rolling into sight. It was an oil delivery truck, but it was longer than it should have been, and taller. On the roof of the truck, on top of the big tank of oil, were two over-sized latches, like those on a suitcase. From between the latches rose a giant handle.

The windows of the truck's cab were dark with many heads; it was packed with people. Teenaged boys stuck their heads out the windows. They raised their mittened hands in the air, and each of them held a bottle of beer. The horn grew louder, filling the air with its piercing noise. The voices of the boys in the cab rose along with the noise of the horn, but what they were saying was incomprehensible.

At a bend in the road, the oil truck turned onto the ice. I looked at the mother and her children, but they were hypnotized by the truck and could not speak.

The truck began to trace an arc on the ice, coming in their direction, then curving almost parallel to shore. The ice groaned and creaked, breaking under the truck's weight. I understood that if the truck stopped, even if it slowed a little, the ice would buckle and break, and the truck would go crashing through.

"Idiots!" I said. "Idiots!" I shook my fist.

At this, a single head emerged from the truck on a long, silly neck. The head wore a tuque over a shock of black, messy hair, the face below the hair had thick, heavy features. The neck extended until the face pressed into mine. "Keep your head covered," the head said. In an instant the neck retracted, and the head was indistinguishable once more inside the truck.

The boy and the younger girl moved in toward shore as the truck approached. The older girl skated in my direction. The mother appeared frozen. She hadn't moved since the truck had come onto the ice. The truck was tracing its arc in her direction, moving closer. "This way!" I shouted, fear rising in my voice. I waved my arms at the mother and turned to skate for the other side of the lake, as an example of what she should do.

The words had barely passed my lips when the ice groaned heavily behind me, followed by a monstrous splashing sound.

When I turned back, the truck and the woman were gone. A black circle of water marked the spot where they had plunged through.

"Mama!" the children screamed in unison. I rounded the edge of the dark water, and rushed to their side. The younger girl and the boy were turning from their sister to the hole in the ice, their faces white.

I told them not to move, and approached the edge of the hole. All the possibilities of action flashed through my mind in succession, like a winter safety film: taking off my belt, getting a branch to extend my reach, removing my own skates so I wouldn't sink if I went into the water.

Already it's too late, I thought. I had a vision of the woman on the other side of the ice, moving slowly against the dark, terrible water, heavy coat on her back, skates on her feet pulling her down, down. She's gone now, I told myself as

I knelt at the edge of the ice. I'll put my face into this icy water, and when I open my eyes all I will see is black. She is dead. She is drowned. She is gone.

I jolted awake in bed. Sweat chilled my face in the cold air. Light came through the window and traced a crazy triangle across the wall. Who is that down there? I wondered, still half dreaming.

I lay in bed with my eyes wide open. I was afraid to go back to sleep, back to that hole in the ice. I knew that if I went back to the edge of that hole, I'd have to look into the water. I'd have to strip off my skates and heavy clothes and plunge into that icy darkness. Who knew what I might find down there?

A murky image wavered at the back of my mind: someone sinking in the cold, cold water. The arms and legs moved languidly through the motions of walking — slowly reaching ahead, then pulling back. The figure was close enough that I felt an urge to reach for it. But I knew it was far away, and moving in the opposite direction.

Hortense meowed plaintively as I rolled over, and for the briefest instant I thought I heard you speak my name. I reached to my head and realized I'd lost my tuque. Frantically I felt around in the bed, and when I found it I pulled it firmly down to my ears.

I rose from the bed and went to the window. It had snowed while I was asleep, and though it had now stopped, enough had collected on the ground to sprinkle everything, except for a few dark patches, with white.

A light bounced suddenly off the neighbour's windows, then spread across the snow on the ground. A large vehicle pulled into the driveway, crunching gravel as it came to a stop. It was an oil truck.

I felt my breath quicken with excitement as a man emerged from the cab, walked to the back of the truck, and began rolling out a long hose. The man wore mukluks, leather mitts, a down-filled coat, and a big, tasselled tuque. I was sure it was the same oil man who had spoken to me earlier. I ran out of the bedroom, along the hallway, and down the stairs, so excited I lost a skate guard in my haste and had to stop to refasten it to my blade.

I needed to talk to that oil man. I wanted to invite him inside for a cup of coffee and thank him for the good advice he'd given me. I wanted to tell him he was right, the head is a chimney, through which everything tries to escape.

• THE NAME EVERYBODY CALLS ME

When Frick raised his eyes again, the road appeared as a mirage, a quavering film of light. In the dark ditch ahead, he thought he saw something: a flash of white. He slowed the car a little. The rain was coming so hard he couldn't see where the road ended and the ditch began. The light from his headlamps slid across the water on the road, leaving the pavement beneath it black. Suddenly there was a flash before him. He jumped on the brake pedal. As the car slid sideways to a stop, there was a sound like a gunshot. Something white rolled across the hood.

"Blessed Jesus!" Frick cried. The engine had stalled. Rain pounded the car.

There's something dead out there, he thought. He slumped forward, his arms arched over the steering wheel, his face on the backs of his hands. There's something dead out there, and I'm going to have to look at it. He considered restarting the car and driving off, not checking the place on the ground by his front wheel, where he knew whatever he'd hit was lying. But he couldn't leave. He'd been almost stopped when he'd struck it, whatever it was. It might still be alive. Even if it was dead, he should pull it to the side of the road, so it wouldn't present a hazard to the next driver.

He braced himself and opened the door. He felt his shoes dampen and become heavy as he stepped onto the roadway. The wind swept up from the bottom of the hill, sending the rain before it in torrents. There wasn't another car in sight.

He stepped around the open door and looked to the ground, at the uneven square of light coming from the interior lamp. Something lay on the pavement, covered with a torn, blood-stained cloth, breathing. He leaned over and touched it. In the cold rain, it felt warm.

Frick laid his foot on top of the thing and rolled it sideways. At the end next to him, an upside-down face appeared in a mat of knotted hair. The eyes blinked and lolled about in their sockets. The mouth, smeared with dirt and blood, opened and closed. "You son of a bitch!" the mouth shrieked. The voice was distorted with emotion, but was unmistakably that of a young girl. The hands shot out at Frick and raked at his face. Frick jumped back, his heart pounding.

The girl leapt to her feet and began running for the woods. Frick bolted after her, catching her at the bottom of the ditch, the two of them tumbling in weeds as the girl screamed and resisted him.

"It's okay. It's okay," Frick said. With one arm, he held the girl by the waist while he tried to keep back her flailing arms with his other hand.

"You son of a bitch!" the girl screeched as he carried her up the bank. By the time they reached the car, the girl had stopped screaming and struggling. She went limp in Frick's arms and was completely silent when he laid her on the back seat. He checked her neck for a pulse and shook her shoulders to see if she was merely asleep. She stirred and mumbled. Her eyes lolled, then she was gone again. He looked her over for signs of her impact with the car — a lump, a bruise, or an indication of a broken bone — but decided that the car must have been almost completely stopped by the time he'd struck her.

But she was a horror to look at. She must have been crawling through the thick brush for hours, perhaps days. Her body was covered with tiny abrasions. There were small, round marks on her inner thighs that looked like cigarette burns. On the backs of her thighs were dark red bruises, as though she'd been beaten with a stick. The hem at the back of her nightdress was soaked with blood. A dark raspberry abrasion marked the middle of her forehead, and one cheek was swollen so large there appeared to be a fist inside it, pushing out from beneath the skin.

There was a rattling noise, and Frick jumped back, slamming his head into the roof of the car. The girl had begun shivering violently in her sleep, her teeth chattering and the backs of her knees drumming the seat.

"Don't, don't!" Frick said stupidly. He put his hands out to steady her, but she continued trembling. He looked in the back seat for something to cover her, but there was nothing. He unbuttoned his wool cardigan, then carefully-removed her tattered nightie and let it fall to the floor. There were dark bruises on her ribs on either side, and the tiny buds of her little breasts had both been burned in the same manner as her thighs. He lifted her gently and felt a row of raw, open wounds on her thin back as he pulled the wool sweater over her torso. In a moment, her shivering became less violent and settled into a mild tremor. Her teeth rattled quietly.

He turned the heater on full as he drove toward town. The rain subsided a little, and the outline of the highway became clear. As he thought about the condition the girl was in, his heartbeat rose in his ears. His hands clutched the steering wheel tightly. He found himself clenching his teeth. Tears rose and receded in his eyes.

"What time is it, Mister?"

Frick jumped in his seat. He looked into the rearview mirror and saw an outline of the girl's ragged hair against the back window.

He stepped on the brake, and when the car had stopped, he turned around in his seat. The girl was sitting bolt upright and smiling at him. When he turned on the interior light, she looked larger and older than she had before.

"How do you feel?" Frick said.

"Fine," the girl said. She laughed.

He laid a hand on her shoulder. Her face twitched. She shrank from his touch.

"Maybe you should lie back down," Frick said.

"I'm not tired," the girl replied.

They were silent a moment. Rain drummed the roof.

"Who did this to you?" Frick said.

"Did what?" the girl said. She smiled at him openly, the dimples in her face bracketing the thin line of her lips. She looked alive now, healthy. So much colour had come into her skin that she appeared luminous.

"What's your name?" Frick asked.

She looked at him coyly. "You want my *real* name?" she asked.

Frick gave her a puzzled look.

"My name's Patricia," she said. "Patricia Works. But everyone calls me Trisha."

"Trisha," Frick said.

"It's nice of you to give me this lift," the girl said. "I don't know what I would have done without it. You can drop me on Orion Avenue in New Glasgow. Do you know where Orion Avenue is?"

"No. I don't," Frick said.

"You know the prefabs?"

Frick nodded.

"It's in the prefabs." Frick turned around and put the car into drive.

"I think we should go to the hospital first," he said. "We can call your parents from the hospital. Is that okay?" He glanced into the mirror. The girl's head had disappeared.

"Trisha?" he said. He turned back around, and the girl was again curled like a fist on the seat, asleep. He watched for the even rise and fall of her shoulders, then continued driving.

The rain had stopped by the time he reached the hospital. The clouds in the night sky had broken. Some stars were visible overhead. He pulled the car into the temporary parking zone in front of the outpatient entrance. Through the glass doors he could see some people waiting in chairs. A large nurse crossed the floor in the direction of the emergency desk.

Frick stepped outside the car and opened the rear door. Trisha's shoulder jerked as he knelt over her. She bounced from the seat and sprang at him like a wild animal, her hands clawing him, her legs and arms flailing. "You son of a bitch!" she cried.

"Trisha. Trisha," he said. "Careful now. You're hurt." He grasped her about the waist with one hand and pushed himself out of the car with the other. He tried to move his free hand under her arms, but she was struggling and flailing too wildly. He had to use one hand to ward off her blows.

She slipped from his grasp and hit the pavement on her feet. As soon as she was free, she bolted across the parking lot, naked but for his cardigan.

He ran after her.

"Trisha! Trisha!" he called. "You're hurt!"

He'd almost caught her before she reached the main lot, but once squeezed between two cars in the first row, she ducked down and disappeared from sight. He ran from row to row and car to car, looking under and between cars as he went, but it was useless. She could hide from him all night here.

The nurse at the emergency desk had short grey and brown hair cut in bangs across the top of her face. Her breasts were the size of loaves of bread. Her white uniform bunched up a roll of fat under each arm. She sat at a desk with a microphone near her mouth. There was a thick plate of glass in front of her with a hole in the middle of it for her to speak through. At the bottom of the glass there was a space to pass papers through. She closed a big novel as Frick approached.

"There is an injured girl in the parking lot," Frick told her. The nurse shifted between the arms of her chair and pushed a button under her desk.

After a few seconds, a security guard came through a door behind her. His big belly pushed out from between a thin pair of black suspenders. He was holding a coffee cup with a Mountie's head on it. *Medicine Hat Alberta* was written under the Mountie. The guard took a drink and set the cup on the nurse's desk.

"This is Mr. Waltzberg," the nurse said. She told Waltzberg what Frick had told her.

Waltzberg spoke in a high-pitched, scratchy voice, the voice of a cartoon character, Frick thought. "Can you describe the girl?" he said.

Frick considered the girl a moment. Her most striking features were the marks and bruises on her body.

"She's small," he said. "Dark hair. She's wearing a cardigan and nothing else. She's been beaten. Tortured."

The guard nodded and walked down a long hall that led away from the emergency ward.

Frick turned away from the nurse and regarded the outpatient area. He longed to find a spot on one of the upholstered benches there and rest.

"Sir? Sir?"

He turned around. The nurse had a form on the desk before her and was holding a pen at the ready to fill it out.

"Name?" she said.

"Frick," he said. "Michael Frick."

"The *girl's* name," the nurse said.

"What's this?" Frick asked. He pointed at the paper the nurse was holding.

"Just the regular form," the nurse replied.

Frick regarded her a moment. "Trisha. Patricia Works," he said at last.

"Address?"

"New Glasgow." Frick thought a moment. "Orion Avenue," he said. "I think."

The nurse pursed her lips. "Number?"

"No idea."

She looked at him.

"Phone?"

"No idea."

The nurse winced. She put a hand on a big hip. "No idea," she said.

"None," Frick said.

"Relationship?" the nurse said.

Frick leaned into the glass that separated them. *"Relationship?"* he said.

The nurse sighed in exasperation. "What is your relationship to the girl?"

"None," Frick said.

"I see," the nurse said. She smiled, placed her pen carefully on her desk, and folded her arms on the papers in front of her. "Look," she said. "Just what is going on here?"

"I wish I knew," Frick said. "I found her on the highway on this side of Mount Thorn. She's been beaten. Tortured. It's the most horrible thing I've ever seen."

"And just who are *you?*"

"I gave you my name before," Frick said. He gripped the ledge beneath the glass. He tightened his hold until his knuckles hurt. The girl was out there in the cold somewhere. Perhaps she'd passed out again.

"Do you have some ID?" the nurse said.

"ID!" Frick said. He pulled the wallet from his back pocket and slammed it on the counter before him. He fumbled through it and took out his driver's licence, thrust it through the hole in the glass.

The nurse snatched up his licence, then reached into her desk and pulled out another form. She started copying information from his licence onto the new form. When Frick craned up his neck to get a look at the form, she angled it away from him, pulling a forearm over what she was writing.

Frick shook his head and walked away from the nurse. "One . . . two . . . three . . . four . . ." he said aloud.

As he took a seat in the waiting room, the security guard, two orderlies, and a man who might have been a doctor walked past, all carrying flashlights. The sight of the four men charging across the outpatient area so purposefully struck Frick as funny. He snickered to himself, then immediately felt guilty. He thought of the wretched little girl outside and shivered with horror. What would have happened, he wondered, if she hadn't run out in front of his car like that? She might have been lost in those woods all night. She would have died of exposure.

Directly across from him sat a man with a blood-soaked towel pressed to his forearm. The man had short grey hair. He wore green work pants and a work shirt, all stained with fresh, dark blood. The woman beside the man in green wore a blue dress with an apron over it. There were no visible marks on her, but she was rocking forward and back, moaning. She sat up straight, then leaned over, put her elbows on her knees, dug her fingers into her scalp, and hissed through clenched teeth.

Misery, Frick thought. He stood up and walked down a passageway, through a glass door to a foyer. He put a loonie into a Coke machine and pressed a button for Coca-Cola Classic. Nothing happened. He slammed the button with the heel of his hand and rocked the machine with his shoulder. It did not respond. He pulled at the coin return lever and the loonie clanged into the coin return slot. He was putting the loonie back into the machine when he noticed his mistake. The price was written beside the coin return lever. One dollar and twenty-five cents.

"A buck and a quarter for a Coke!" Frick exclaimed. He looked over his shoulder for a witness to this injustice. Through the glass door and down the long hall behind him, the woman in the blue dress stood up, put her palms to her forehead, and leaned back with her mouth open, as though she were screaming. He listened a moment, but heard nothing. He dug the extra quarter from his pocket and took a can of Coke from the machine.

He drank down the contents of the can in several long drinks. The acid liquid burned at his stomach, but with some sugar and caffeine in him, he felt better.

The nurse looked directly at him when he re-entered the outpatient area, but instead of signalling to him, she pushed a button on her desk, leaned into the microphone near her, and announced to the whole room:

"Mr. Frick, please. Mr. Frick."

When Frick arrived at her desk, she slid his licence through the slot in the glass.

"What did you say that girl's name was?" the nurse asked. Frick threw up his arms. "You know what I said her name was," he said. "You wrote it down."

"Works?" the nurse asked. "W-O-R-K-S?"

"Patricia Works," Frick replied.

"And the address?" asked the nurse.

"Look," said Frick. The Coke was burning in his stomach. "What are you trying to get at?"

"Well," said the nurse. She shuffled a stack of papers on her desk. "I called a Mr. and Mrs. Jim Works on Orion Avenue in New Glasgow. Twelve Orion Avenue."

"Twelve," said Frick. "I told you I didn't know the number."

"I asked Mrs. Works if they had a daughter Patricia," the nurse continued. "She said yes. When I told her the girl was here and she was injured, the woman hung up on me. I called back and she hung up again. The third time I phoned, the woman told me her daughter was home in front of the TV."

Frick stared at the nurse. "Is there another Works on Orion Avenue?" he asked.

The nurse shook her head.

"Well, I don't know who the girl is. But she said her name was Trisha Works from Orion Avenue."

The nurse nodded and smiled. "Thank you, Mr. Frick," she said. "There's no need for you to wait here. We have your name and address, and if our people outside do find anything, the police will know where to find you for questioning."

"Listen," said Frick. "There's a little girl out there. A little girl in desperate condition." He pointed a finger at the door to the parking lot, and as he did so, the doctor and two orderlies came through, headed by Waltzberg, the security guard.

Their expressions were blank. Their long flashlights drooped toward the floor. The orderlies and the doctor kept walking through the emergency ward and into the hospital. The security guard stopped and addressed the nurse. "We can't find anything," he squeaked. "We checked the whole parking lot. Under and around every car. We checked the graveyard nextdoor. We even went down to the river-bank. There's nothing out there."

"You're giving up already!" Frick said. "That girl's going to die of exposure." He turned to the nurse. "You'd better call the police."

The nurse frowned and chewed at her lip.

"Mr. Frick," she said. "I appreciate your worry. But we only call the police in dire circumstances."

Frick's eyes widened. "Dire circumstances!" he said.

"I'm sorry, Mr. Frick. But this is an emergency room. We deal with emergencies every day. I have very specific instructions about when I am to call the police, or else we'd have the police here every minute. Mr. Waltzberg here," she motioned at the security guard, "is a retired member of the New Glasgow police force. I'm sure if Mr. Waltzberg can't find anything, there would be nothing the police could do. We have a lot of faith in Mr. Waltzberg." She smiled at the security guard. The guard pulled shyly at his belt.

"Do you think I'm making this up?" Frick said. "Do you think I'm some sort of fruit cake?"

"Look," said the nurse. "I have my job to do. I have my instructions to follow. I am to call the police in dire circumstances. I don't see any dire circumstances. I've already upset a woman over on Orion Avenue tonight. On *your* advice," she paused significantly, looking askance at Frick. "If you want to call the police yourself, you are free to do so." She stopped talking and folded her arms across her chest.

"I will, then," Frick said. He reached through the hole in the glass for the phone. The nurse put her big hand on the receiver. "There are pay phones in the front entrance," she said.

Frick twisted his face in anger, piercing her with his stare.

He charged to the front entrance and stood before the pay phones a moment, breathing deeply to calm himself. The police number was displayed beneath a sheet of clear plastic on the front of the phone.

"New Glasgow Police Department, may I help you?" The

voice on the other end was a high-pitched squeal.

"What's going on here!" Frick barked. "Is that you, Waltzberg?"

"Who the hell is this?" the voice on the other end demanded.

Frick put his hand to his forehead. He knew he was going crazy.

"Who is this?" the policeman said. "Hello! Hello!"

"Shit!" Frick said. He slammed down the receiver and pulled the phone book from the shelf under the phone. There it was: James Works, 12 Orion Avenue, 755-9909. He dialled the number and a woman answered. "Mrs. Works?" Frick said.

"Yes," the woman said, perhaps hesitantly.

"Mrs. Jim Works?"

"Yes." Frick heard a TV in the background.

"Do you have a daughter named Trisha?" His hand tightened on the receiver.

"Is this the hospital again?" The woman's voice thinned. "My husband won't stand for this kind of harassment. Jim! Jim!" she called.

Frick hung up. He laid his forearm against the top of the phone and rested his head against it.

Then he remembered the dress! The bloody and torn nightgown the girl had been wearing when he'd found her. If he brought that to the police he wouldn't have to explain anything. He rushed out of the hospital and into the back seat of his car. He searched on the floor, under the front seats, and down the crack in the back seat, but he couldn't find it. He checked the ledge under the back window. "Damn it!" he said. He checked again in all the places he'd already looked, then checked places he knew it wasn't: the glove compartment, even the trunk. He was looking behind a rear wheel when a dark figure appeared in the corner of his eye. He looked up. It was Waltzberg. He was holding a cheap blue pen over an open notebook.

"This is a five minute patient drop off and pick up only zone," Waltzberg squeaked. He pointed at a sign on a metal post. "You'll have to leave or I'll ticket you. I can do that, you know. I can ticket."

It didn't take long to locate Orion Avenue once he was in the prefabs in the North End of New Glasgow. It was a short side street that ran along the base of a steep hill. Frick drove to the end of it, stopping in front of number twelve. The house was a prefab bungalow, like all the other houses in the neighbourhood. It was white with black false shutters at either end of the two windows that faced the street. Through the picture window came the dim, shifting light of TV. The other window was dark. In the driveway, under the glow of a floodlight, stood a faded metallic-blue Chev.

He sat in his car and watched the light that flickered in the window for some sign of human movement. None came. Just the shifting and flickering of day scenes followed by night scenes followed by commercials.

He left his car and stood on the narrow sidewalk before the house. There were few streetlights nearby, and over-head, the leafless branches of trees rattled against each other in the wind. He walked across the dead grass of the lawn and stepped onto the front step. The doorbell had been painted over, and he guessed it hadn't worked in years. He bent down and tapped lightly, but audibly, at the alumi-num panel below his knees. Almost immediately he heard a quick, gentle thumping of footsteps. The inside door opened. "Trisha!" Frick said. He opened the aluminum door and stepped inside. The girl moved aside to let him in, but stared up at him with a questioning look. There could be no doubt. This was the same girl. She looked healthier than she had looked in his car earlier, not so gaunt. Her cheek, once swollen like a fist, was now back to its regular size. The nightdress she wore looked like the one he'd removed from her himself when he'd given her his sweater, but it was clean and pressed and not tattered in the least. Her hair was washed and combed and had a healthy sheen. It was done up in a braid at either side. On her face and arms there did not appear a single blemish, except a slight reddish mark in the centre of her forehead, where there had been a fresh abrasion only a few hours before.

The girl looked at him blankly, and Frick looked blankly at her.

"Trisha," he said again.

"Trisha?" came a woman's voice from the hallway behind the girl. "Trisha?"

The woman looked at Frick and gasped. She put a hand on the girl's shoulder and drew her back.

"Something's going on here," Frick said.

"Jim! Jim!" the woman called. "Come quick!"

There were heavy thumps on the floor. A slim, solid-looking man appeared beside the woman.

"What's going on here?" the man asked.

"I might ask that same question," Frick said. He looked the man up and down.

"What the hell are you saying?" the man said. His voice was deep and powerful. He stepped forward and confronted Frick directly. His hair was short and neat. His face was square, handsome, though his cheeks sagged a little with the first signs of age.

"I want you to know something," Frick said. He looked the man in the face. "I want you to know that I know. No. Not that I know. But there is something," he said. "Something —"

"You son of a bitch," the man said. He grabbed Frick by the collar and pushed him out the door. His fist hit Frick's cheek like a block of stone.

Frick picked himself off the wet lawn and looked back at the man's dark silhouette in the doorway of the house. He made his way back to the car and sat for a moment, touching the side of his face where he'd been hit. He pulled down the rearview mirror and flipped on the interior light to look at his cheek. His skin was flushed with blood and had started to balloon. His lips were red with blood. He poked a finger around inside his mouth and felt the row of holes where his teeth had cut into the flesh.

In a corner of the mirror, he caught sight of something in the back seat. He turned around to find his cardigan, neatly folded. He picked up the sweater by the shoulders and examined it. It was clean and fresh and dry, as if it had just come from the cleaner's. A piece of delicate blue onion-skin paper stuck out of a front pocket. He slipped the paper from the pocket. It had been folded once neatly through the middle. A faint sweet smell came from the paper as he unfolded it and held it up to the light. Written in black in a careful, childish hand was a single word: *Please.*

• A THING LIKE SNOW

Ralph lay far to one side of the double bed. After almost two years, he was still unused to the absence of his wife. He shut his eyes. Only her warm breath, he thought. Today I wish only to feel her warm breath. But he was alone. The only thing behind him, as he lay curled away from the centre of the bed, was the cold side of the mattress.

The power was out. The streetlight out on Hudson Street, when it shone, shone directly through his bedroom window between the small opening he left in the curtains and onto his alarm clock. He heard the metallic clicking of the clock on the nightstand beside him, but he couldn't see it.

He reached out, felt the cold top of the clock in his palm, and pushed in the button on its back. He sighed.

His retirement began today. For the first Monday morning in almost forty years, he had nowhere to go. How long had he and Raylene looked forward to this day, to this very morning? They were supposed to wake up in Florida; that's the way they'd planned it. Nothing to do but eat those big oranges and enjoy the sunshine. They'd been saving for a Winnebago when Raylene had passed on. The money still sat in a Scotiabank term deposit.

He sighed again, then shoved away the quilts. Even through long Johns and flannel pyjamas the cold bit him. The furnace had gone out with the power. Damn that furnace anyway. He had argued and fought with Raylene for years before he had agreed to switch to oil.

"Here we are," he used to say, pointing at the floor of the kitchen. "Here we are sitting on the thickest seam of coal in the world, with nothing but woods as far as you can see. I'll be Jesus damned before we piss our money away to the A-rabs."

Each year the cold on winter mornings got harder on them both. The trips down the rickety stairway to the cellar, to shovel coal and load wood, were difficult. It had ended with Raylene breaking her hip. They took her to the hospital in an ambulance, and the doctor said the hip would mend. But there were other things, he said. There were things inside her that would not mend. Things that were small, but would only get bigger. And he was right.

He fumbled with his feet on the cold floor before he found his slippers. He put on his robe and went downstairs. The thermostat was set at sixty-five degrees, but the thermometer beneath it read forty-five. Shit, he thought. Soon I'll be seeing my breath in here. He slowly nudged the dial to seventy, then to seventy-five, then to eighty, waiting to hear a roar from the burner in the cellar. Nothing. He put his thumb on the centre of the dial and watched the thermometers needle climb. When it reached sixty, he took his thumb away. He felt better, as though he had staved off the chill for a while.

Out the kitchen window, under the fading light of stars, the neighbourhood lay drifted with snow. The peaked roofs of old company houses jutted out of nothing but snowdrifts. Now he remembered waking through the night and hearing the storm. The wind had howled over the chimney. The windows had rattled. All that turmoil could have been a dream in the calm this morning, the sky clear overhead.

The snowed-in houses were as blank to Ralph as the lives of their occupants. At one time, he had known every person in every house. Each house had had a family, and each family a history. Right to this day he could remember his old paper route, which houses took both the *Herald* in the morning and the *News* at night, and which houses took only one or the other.

Jobs had been stable then. Wages weren't much, but a person could depend on them. Now that was shot to hell. Nobody stayed put; they went to where the jobs were: Quebec, Ontario, and farther west. They pulled up their families and left. Anyone in the neighbourhood now was in transit, touching down in Albion Mines as just another small town near a shaky job that might soon disappear.

While Raylene was alive, the neighbouring houses had not seemed so foreign. Someone was always dropping by.

Kids were always knocking at the door to see if they could make a dollar doing some little chore. The phone was always ringing. Ralph had had the impression that he and Raylene were connected, that they had friends, that they were part of a community. Raylene had known how to treat the neighbourhood kids so they would come back. She knew how to talk to people over the phone so they called again. She had a way of making people feel welcome when they arrived at the door so that they wanted to return. It had not taken long after Raylene died for Ralph to realize that the hive of human interaction that was their house while Raylene was alive had been the day-to-day product of her personality. Without her there to continuously breathe life into their relationships with people in the neighbourhood, those relationships soon deflated and died.

The tip of Ralph's nose touched the cold pane of the window, startling him out of his reverie and leaving a small greasy circle on the glass. Across the alley, old Mrs. Simpson's house was drifted nearly to the downstairs windows. But the new people who had moved in there were already up and had shovelled the step. They had the kitchen stove going. Snow had melted away from the base of the chimney. Smoke rose straight in the still, clear air.

Hippies, he called those people, though nobody called themselves Hippies anymore, if they ever had. Ralph didn't like the look of the Hippies. The Mister had hair over his shoulders and a beard. The Missus wore no makeup, no bra. Their two kids got around in gum rubbers. The whole crew of them wore baggy clothes and ponytails. God only knew what they'd be growing in the backyard come spring.

It was the Hippies' backyard that had turned Ralph against them. Poor old Mrs. Simpson hadn't gardened there in years. What had been the garden when Mr. Simpson was alive had grown over with grass. The only thing remaining was the rhubarb patch, a thick swath of plants that grew right up alongside the house.

For the first few years after Mr. Simpson's death, Ralph and Raylene watched out their kitchen window as the rhubarb grew thick and healthy in the summer, turned overgrown and woody by fall, and eventually rotted into the ground.

On the third summer, as the stalks grew thick, Ralph approached Mrs. Simpson and asked her would she mind if he picked some rhubarb. He'd give her half of what he harvested.

He stood on the old woman's back step. She stood in the doorway. The smell of her closed-up house poured out the door.

"Take it all if you like. I've got no use for it," she said. "Poor Jim loved his rhubarb pie, but since he's gone I don't bother with it. Don't care for it at all myself."

Each year after that Raylene baked pies and made jam. What she and Ralph couldn't eat themselves brought in a few dollars at the Sunday flea market.

After Raylene had passed on, Ralph looked for recipes in her old cookbooks. That fall he baked the pies and boiled the jam himself, thinking of her. The rich tangy smell brought back the greyness of her hair in the kitchen, the flour on her strong hands. He carried out her cooking for her like the subtle rituals of a religion. He even set up a booth at the flea market, with a sign that read *Raylene's Famous Rhubarb Confections.* He'd planned to make it an annual affair.

Then last spring Mrs. Simpson died. Ralph had first known her as a customer on his paper route. She had taken both the *News* and the *Herald,* and he thought of her all his adult life as a good tipper, and as a woman who would give him pudding at Christmas. Even though he had never been inside her house — knew her mostly as a shadow that passed before the curtained windows in the night, a hunched form calling the cats into the house in the morning — she had been a fixture in the neighbourhood, something unchanging.

She had children in Ontario, he knew. A man and a woman in their fifties, married, and with grown children of their own. All summer, figuring they'd show up sooner or later to divide up the property and sell the place, Ralph took care to mow the lawn and occasionally water the rhubarb.

In the end, no Simpson came to reclaim the house. One morning Ralph noticed in the street a large moving truck with New Brunswick plates. Two heavy-set young men in coveralls emptied the house of Mrs. Simpson's belongings: big, old chesterfields and stuffed chairs. A china cabinet which, even empty, the two young movers could barely budge between them.

As he watched the full truck start down the street, Ralph thought about the empty house across from his. Alone, he thought. Now I'm alone. He said the word aloud and imagined it echoing in the hollow rooms of the Simpson place.

The next day when he got up, there was a white Volkswagen van in the Simpson driveway. The Hippies had arrived.

He had never seen the Hippies load furniture or any belongings into the house. He imagined them inside in empty rooms, sleeping on the floor in sleeping bags. Maybe they were nudists and wore no clothes indoors. Back to nature, wasn't that what those people were about?

The Hippies had come just prior to rhubarb harvest. Before Ralph got up enough courage to approach them and tell them the rhubarb technically belonged to him and to the memory of Raylene, it was gone. All of it. All at once. The Hippies had taken it for themselves.

Ralph was hungry. He went to the fridge and opened it. The light did not come on. He leaned in and squinted. The dark outlines of things stood out against white enamel. Raw bacon and raw eggs, he thought. He had nothing to cook on, everything was electric. He closed the fridge.

One by one, he opened the cupboard doors and closed them. Canned goods. Campbell's soup. Beans and corn.

Christ, he thought. Not even a box of cornflakes in the house. He went back to the fridge, filled a glass with milk, and drank it. His stomach growled.

He took a piece of white bread from the bag on top of the fridge and smothered it with peanut butter. He lay the bread flat on his hand, pretending it was toast, and bit off a corner. It stuck to the roof of his mouth. He sat at the table and tried to unstick the peanut butter and bread, opening and closing his mouth like a dog with chewing gum between its teeth. He shivered with the cold and drew his arms around himself. A slight trace of steam exited his mouth.

Just then a knock, clear in the cold air, sounded at the back door.

"Who in Jesus' name," Ralph said aloud. The lump of bread and peanut butter came unstuck. He swallowed it. He set the slice of bread on the table, wrapped his robe tightly about him, and walked through the back porch. The porch smelled like the heavy coats that hung on nails against the wall.

The door pushed up a pile of snow as he opened it. Some dim rays of morning glinted in his eyes. A figure in snowshoes, gum rubbers, melton wool pants, parka, and scarf stood on the buried doorstep. A second pair of snowshoes, tails stuck in the snow, stood behind.

"For the love of Christ," said Ralph, stepping back from the door to clear the way. "Come in, come in, whoever you are."

The figure bent down, flicked off the snowshoe bindings and stepped inside. Ralph shut the door and waved his guest into the kitchen.

"Well," he said. He stood for a moment with his hands in front of him defensively. The figure's head was covered by the parka hood, a scarf wrapped around at mouth level. The hood came so far forward over the face that Ralph could not see the figure's eyes.

The figure said something.

"What's that, now?" Ralph said, and leaned cautiously forward.

A mittened hand poked out of a parka sleeve and unwrapped the scarf, then pulled down the hood. It was a Hippie kid. The boy. Ralph had never seen him up this close. He put the boy at fourteen, fifteen years old. A short, blond ponytail stuck out the back of his tuque. His cheekbones were high, his complexion ruddy from the cold. His two steely blue eyes pierced into Ralph like ice-picks.

Ralph stepped back. For a moment he thought the boy might rob him.

"I'm sorry," the boy said. "I'm your neighbour from across." He pointed a thumb over his shoulder. "My parents sent me here to check on you, make sure you're okay."

Ralph heard an accent when the boy spoke, but he couldn't place it.

"I'm all right," said Ralph. He pulled the open neck of his robe closed. "I'm okay. Power off everywhere?"

"Guess so," said the boy. He blew out a pale cloud of breath. "You got no heat here?"

"Aw, the damn furnace," said Ralph. He gestured toward the thermostat.

The boy looked at the bread and peanut butter on the table.

"Come over to our place," he said. "We've got the stove going."

"No, there's no need of that, now," Ralph said. He waved his hand through the air like he was fanning away a bad smell. "No need of that at all."

"It's no trouble," the boy said. "My parents said." The boy looked at Ralph's robe. "I'll wait for you to get dressed."

"Now, there's no need." Ralph stood his ground for a moment.

"I've got a pair of snowshoes here for you and everything," the boy said. He motioned to the door. He looked at Ralph. "We're expecting you," he said.

"Well," Ralph said.

The boy sat at the table.

The crisp air caught in Ralph's lungs as they walked out the back door. It was lighter out, but not yet light. His nostril hairs froze. The Hippie boy put on his snowshoes and lay the pair he had brought for Ralph flat on the snow.

"Been years since I wore a pair of these," said Ralph. "On my paper route. Don't know that I'll remember how."

The boy bent to adjust Ralph's bindings for him. "You just walk," he said. "Like this."

The boy walked ahead of him, steady and sure-footed. Ralph dragged his heavy feet. The snow beneath him squeaked. The scent of the Hippies' wood smoke sweetened the air.

Ralph and the boy stopped by the back porch door, removed their snowshoes, and leaned them against the painted clapboard. They banged snow off their boots before they entered the house.

"Welcome! Welcome! Welcome!." It was Mr. Hippie who spoke. His coarse, blond hair hung to his shoulders, his beard was thick. He had tiny, sunken eyes, and a long nose. He stood at the doorway between the porch and the kitchen and waved Ralph in.

Ralph took off his boots, parka, tuque, and scarf. He entered the Hippie kitchen after the boy.

A wave of heat swept over him. It was woodstove heat, it had a taste and a texture. It was a heat Ralph had grown unused to. His face flushed. The tight skin beneath his clothes loosened. His pores opened and he began to sweat. Across the room he saw a Keymac stove with a warming oven. The enamel, though pitted with black chips in several places, gleamed. On the stovetop lay several pans and pots, covered with inverted pie plates. Behind the stove, stacked in a neat pile, stood wedges of what looked like maple. A refrigerator sat mute beside the wood, a mute transistor radio on its top. A faint glow from outside was slowly beginning to halo the windows, but most of the light in the room came from an old-fashioned kerosene lamp that stood beside the radio.

"Are you okay?" said Mr. Hippie. "You're turning red."

Ralph's eyes watered. He looked at Mr. Hippie. Mr. Hippie pulled a wooden chair away from the kitchen table and Ralph sat.

"Now that's a fire," Ralph said.

Mr. Hippie smiled. "Enough snow for you?" he said. He laughed loudly.

Ralph shifted in his seat.

"Tommit," Mr. Hippie said, and stuck out his hand at Ralph.

"What?" said Ralph, thinking he was hearing a foreign language. He shrunk from the hand.

"Hi," said Mr. Hippie, his hand still extended. He had an accent like the boy's, but thicker. "We've never been introduced. My name's Tommit. You've met my son, Jana." He nudged his head toward the boy, who stood near the stove, warming himself.

"All right," Ralph said. "All right. Tommit." Tommit and Jana, he thought. And Jana is a boy. He stood and offered Mr. Hippie his hand. They squeezed each other's fingers solidly.

"Ralph," said Ralph.

"Ralph," said Mr. Hippie. "My wife'll be down in a minute, Ralph. She's getting our daughter out of bed. Day off school. You know. Then we'll have a breakfast."

"Don't go to no trouble, now," said Ralph. "I told your boy here. Don't be going to no trouble over me. I'll just sit here in the warm till the power comes on."

"It's no trouble," Mr. Hippie said. "We eat breakfast every morning!" He slapped his knee hard and bent over laughing.

What the hell was that? thought Ralph. What kind of dope can this man be on to produce an outburst like that?

"It's a joke," said Mr. Hippie, as though he had read Ralph's mind. "It's only a joke."

"A joke," said Ralph. He forced a smile.

"No work today?" said Mr. Hippie. "Too much snow?"

"Retired," said Ralph.

"Well, that's something," said Mr. Hippie.

"We'll see," said Ralph. "We'll see what it is. You?"

"Retired?" said Mr. Hippie. He laughed again.

"No work?" said Ralph.

Mr. Hippie shrugged. "Like you say," he said. "We'll see." Just then the woman, Mrs. Hippie, came into the kitchen. Her long, lustreless, blond hair was pulled back into a pony tail. She wore a white T-shirt beneath bib overalls. Her face was square as a block of wood, and she smiled at Ralph with giant teeth. "Ralph," said Mr. Hippie, rising from his seat. "This is Leitha. Leitha, this is our neighbour, Ralph."

"Glad to meet you, Lisa," said Ralph. He stood and half-extended his arm, not knowing if it was proper to offer this woman his hand.

"Leitha," said Mrs. Hippie. She gripped Ralph's hand. Her fingers were calluses and hard bone. "Leitha. It's a common mistake." She too had an accent. She held Ralph's hand firmly until he no longer felt her calluses, only her warmth.

"A common mistake?" said Ralph.

"My name," Mrs. Hippie said. "And this is the man," she continued, holding Ralph's hand and fixing him with her stare. "This is the man who has his laundry hung before we're out of bed on Saturday."

Ralph felt as though he were being accused of something. "O-only in the warm weather," he said.

"*Only in the warm weather!*" said Mrs. Hippie. She pumped his hand up, then down, and released it. She laughed. She went to Mr. Hippie and kissed him on the lips.

"Is she coming down, or do we start without her?" Mr. Hippie said. "Our guest is hungry."

Before Ralph could say anything, Mrs. Hippie said, "She'll be down." She rubbed her upper arms with her palms. "It's still quite cold up there. I had to convince her it was warmer down here." She picked a coffee perker off the stove, and with it filled a large mug which she set on the table.

"Sit back down now, Ralph," she said. She placed her big hand on Ralph's shoulder and applied gentle pressure. "Drink some coffee. Come away from the fire, Jana. You'll toast yourself." The boy turned from the stove, and the four of them sat simultaneously at the table.

"Would you like cream or sugar?" Mr. Hippie said.

"It's fine," Ralph said. He wrapped his hands about the cup. He took a sip and felt the hot liquid burn slowly into him. "Ah," he said. "Good coffee. Haven't had perked coffee, coffee perked in a perker, in a long time."

"Justice Juice," said Mr. Hippie. He smiled.

"What's that, now?" said Ralph.

"It's Bridgehead," said Mrs. Hippie. "The coffee."

Ralph looked at her.

"Daddy calls it Justice Juice," said the boy.

Ralph remained silent.

Mr. Hippie leaned forward and punched Ralph on the shoulder with the end of his fist.

"Justice Juice," he said. "That's a good one, eh?"

Ralph took another drink. "It's good," he said.

When the girl came in, everyone looked up. She was around ten or eleven. She had her mother's square face, but there was something of her father in her sunken eyes, and also in the shape of her nose. She wore baggy flannel pyjamas.

"Tadjat, this is our neighbour, Ralph," said Mrs. Hippie. The girl smiled briefly.

"Tadjat!" Ralph exclaimed. Immediately he regretted it. He lowered his head and looked at his hands. A lump rose in his throat. He looked up.

"It was my mother's name," said Mr. Hippie. "May she

rest in peace." The whole family made a quick gesture that could have been the sign of the cross.

"I'm . . . I'm . . ." said Ralph. He had no idea what to say. The girl had not been offended. She pulled out a chair for herself at the table.

"Well, it's breakfast time," said Mr. Hippie. He got up, plucked an apron from the back of his seat, and tied it around his waist. He opened the warming oven and took out two large tins of muffins. A tart smell filled the room.

Steam rose into Mr. Hippie's face. Mrs. Hippie and both kids rubbed their tummies. They said in unison: "Mmm."

Ralph got first choice of muffins. He selected a small one. "Mmm," he said. He turned to Mrs. Hippie. "Smells like good muffins you made."

"Tommit made them," the woman answered.

Ralph broke open the muffin. It crumbled perfectly away from itself. "Tommit made them," he said. A swirl of steam curled for an instant between the two halves. The squarish chunks on the inside were as unmistakable as the invigorating smell.

"Rhubarb muffins," Ralph said.

"Daddy's rhubarb," said the girl.

"If you don't like rhubarb, I won't mind if you don't eat it. There's plenty else here. We have bread, and I've got porridge coming up," said Mr. Hippie.

"Listen," said Ralph. "I *love* rhubarb."

"Well, there's been no shortage of rhubarb in this household. We've got more of it out back than we know what to do with. Next summer, feel free to help yourself."

Ralph looked at Mr. Hippie.

Mr. Hippie smiled.

Ralph had never tasted rhubarb in a muffin before. He

ate the first half slowly, cautiously, savouring each moderate bite. The second half he gobbled, as though all the taste of all the rhubarb in the world were in it. He reached for another. He split this one in two, buttered it, and ate slowly, though in big bites.

When he had finished, he sat back for a moment.

"He *does* like rhubarb," said the boy. He turned his head so all could see him smiling. Everyone laughed, including Ralph.

Ralph looked at the table where Mr. Hippie had set out the meal. Aside from the large plate of muffins, there was homemade bread and biscuits. Red River cereal steamed in a crock container. There were hot scrambled eggs, a sausage roll, and a tub of crunchy peanut butter. Slices of tomato and cucumber lay on a separate plate.

The Hippie family lowered their heads and ate. They ate in earnest. They leaned into it as though it was a chore, and they concentrated. Ralph listened for a moment to their diligent chewing, their breathing, and the clank of silverware on plates and bowls. They ate like guiltless, honest, happy people, he thought. He joined them.

When they had finished, Leitha made a fresh pot of coffee and filled Ralph's mug again.

"Oh my, oh my," Ralph said. He rubbed his belly. "Oh boy, oh my, oh my."

"Glad you enjoyed it," said Tommit.

"You'll have to come over often," said Leitha. "Tommit could use some encouragement about his cooking. We're all so spoiled in this family."

Tommit went red.

The children sat fidgeting in their chairs.

"Tadjat, you'll have to get dressed, now. Get dressed and start your day," said Leitha. "Jana, could you put more wood on the fire, please? For dishes."

Tadjat ran upstairs, thumping her feet soundly as she went. As Jana lifted the stove lid, the fridge jittered, then began to hum.

"Power's on," said Tommit. He rose and dimmed the kerosene lamp, then flicked on the electric light with the switch.

Ralph looked at the shivering fridge. It occurred to him that if the fridge hadn't come on, he could have sat in that kitchen forever.

"Oh, I should go, then," he said.

"No, no. Do stay," said Leitha.

"You've only just arrived," said Tommit.

Ralph rose slowly. He was silent for a moment.

"No. No," he said. "I've got stuff to do over there. The furnace." He looked sadly at Leitha and Tommit, then made his way into the porch and got dressed for the walk back. Out the window he saw his own cold chimney cough out the first thin wisps of smoke.

"Use my snowshoes. The ones you came on," said Leitha. "We'll get them next time."

Tommit handed Ralph a small, warm, paper bag.

Ralph uncurled the top of the bag and looked inside.

"Take these muffins," said Tommit. "Eat them."

Outside, the sun glared off the snow and made Ralph squint. He strapped on the snowshoes and turned to look at Tommit and Leithas house. The whole family, all four of them, stood in the window and waved. Through the frost, they smiled.

As he moved across the top of the snow, Ralph was

conscious that he was walking above the ground. He looked to his waist and decided that, if it weren't for this snowfall, that's about where his head would be. A thing like snow can change everything, he thought. Change the entire landscape. He swung his arms as he strode toward his house.

About him the neighbourhood was incapacitated. Most chimneys smoked now, but nothing moved. The roads would not be plowed for hours.

"Hey!" he shouted. The snow soaked up the noise.

He stopped before his back door and leaned the snowshoes against the house. He looked back across his wide tracks in the snow to where his new neighbours lived. Nothing moved behind the small, dark windows. For an instant he imagined he had never been in there. So odd, he thought. But true.

He turned, opened the door, and stepped inside. The porch smelled like the heavy coats that hung on nails against the wall. In the basement, the furnace roared.

• THE TRANSFORMED SKY

"Any fool can see it's an eye," one man said. He pointed at the object, still and shimmering in the sky.

"I think it's a lightbulb," said a woman in curlers. "And that thing just below it," she went on. "I think that's a horse." She had rushed outside from her bedroom when she'd heard the commotion. She'd been talking to her sister Vicki in Toronto, and had hung up on her when she'd heard the screeching tires and cries of surprise.

A policeman rode up on a bicycle. He was gazing so intently at the sky that he almost bumped into a fire hydrant.

"Careful, officer," the woman in curlers said.

"In twenty years on the force . . ." the policeman said.

On all the lawns of Guernica Street and out into the

street itself, dumbstruck people stood, still as grazing cattle, staring at the sky. At the high end of the street, a hill of birches opened into Toro del Sol, where a similar scene was unfolding.

A pealing of bells rang out. A white-bearded man in a white robe came pedalling down Guernica Street on a Dickie Dee ice cream tricycle.

"I have predicted this! I have predicted this!" the man shouted, a palm to the side of his mouth for effect. He stopped his tricycle and opened the lid of the ice box on its front. The box was stacked with books, hundreds of copies of a slim blue paperback. The old man reached down and pulled out a single copy. *The Sky Transformed was* written in yellow on its cover.

"*The Sky Transformed?* the old man said. "Written more than five years ago. That lightbulb up there," he pointed at the sky. "Read about it on page fifty-two."

"I knew it was a lightbulb," the woman in curlers said. She looked about for the man who'd said it was an eye, but she couldn't find him in the crowd that had gathered around the old man and his tricycle.

"Ten dollars!" the man barked above the heads of all around. "Find out what will happen!"

The policeman propped his bicycle on its stand and made his way through the crowd to the old man. People were pushing to get to the front of the line.

"Do you have a permit, sir?" the officer said.

The man reached into his robe and brought out a piece of paper. He unfolded it and handed it to the policeman.

The officer brought out a pair of glasses from his shirt pocket and put them on before examining the paper. "Okay," he said at last. He gave the paper back to the old man and replaced the glasses in the pocket. "Now about these horses," the officer said. He put his hands on his hips and gazed up at the sky.

"Horses!" the old man said. He shook his head and laughed. "Officer," he said, handing over a copy of his book. "This one is free. A man who has dedicated his life to upholding the laws of the land should know."

The policeman accepted the book with a bow and made his way through the crowd to his bicycle. He looked seriously at the book for a moment, turning it over in his hands. He put on his glasses and studied the cover. He put the book in his parcel carrier, mounted his bike, and rode off in the direction of Toro del Sol.

The crowd around the old man's tricycle increased, and the price of the book increased with it. By the time the woman in curlers got to the front of the line, the price had gone from ten to fifteen to twenty dollars. She was lucky enough to get one of the last copies. The old man smiled at her as he handed her the book. His eyes were clear, translucent blue. His lips, fringed with the white moustache and beard, looked like dark strips of meat.

"I can tell you are a good woman," the old man said. "You have a clear conscience. A good heart." He placed a hand on her shoulder as she turned and walked in the direction of her house. She was moved by the sincerity of the old man's words. A lump rose in her throat. Tears welled in her eyes. She blinked them back.

The sky had not changed since the moment it had been transformed, but the crowds had begun to thin. Traffic began flowing again on Guernica Street. The woman looked down at herself in nightgown and slippers. She put a hand to the curlers in her hair. "Lord, look at me!" she said. She ran up the walk to her front door and turned for a last look at the sky before she went inside. If those aren't horses, she thought, I wonder what they are. She looked down at the book in her hands. The price on the cover was three dollars and fifty cents. A chocolate ice cream stain all but obscured the blurb on the back. As she was opening the door, the phone began to ring. "Vicki!" she exclaimed. She rushed inside to answer it.

• IN MY HEART

I called a black man a nigger once. Right to his face. That was the night I got myself thrown out of high school and left that part of my life behind forever. I had been drinking, and what I said, or the part of what I said that stands out most clearly now in my mind, was a single word of an hour-long interaction. And the night I am talking about was one incident of several that had been piling up then, causing my life to change.

I remember what happened, but I do not understand it: why I said what I said. The person I said it to had done nothing to harm me, and I do not believe I felt personal resentment toward him. Maybe what I did has something to do with where and when I grew up: Pictou County, Nova

Scotia, in a town called Albion Mines. When was a while ago. Not that things are different anywhere else or that anything in Albion Mines has changed since then. Not that a single thing has changed.

It was a Friday in September. The school year that was just starting should have been my senior year of high school, but one thing had led to another the year before, and I was repeating grade eleven.

On the first day of classes I had made a pledge to myself that I would stay out of trouble for the whole year. I knew I had screwed up the year before. I would be back in grade eleven for ten more months, and I had nobody to blame but myself. I had had the whole summer to think about what I had done wrong and how I could fix it in the coming year. It was a behaviour problem, they'd said. And so I had made a pledge to myself on the first day of classes, a pledge to change my behaviour. But even though classes had barely begun — we were a week into the regular schedule — things were already coming to a head between me and the principal of Albion Mines High School, a man named Fred Roland.

For the most part, things had gone smoothly during the first week of school. I had missed classes on Tuesday, but that was not the kind of thing that started major trouble. Then on Thursday a teacher reported to Principal Roland that he had smelled cigarette smoke in the bathroom after I had been in there. Cigarette smoke is hard to pin on a person, but that incident told me that I should be careful. The word was out on me.

Then on Friday afternoon, Roland called me into his office. I was sitting in the metal shop before the last period of the day when my name came over the loudspeaker. "Come to the office at three-thirty," was all the secretary said. Then she went on to announce the dance that would take place that night, the first dance of the year.

When the bell rang at three-thirty I was sweeping the floor of the metal shop. I dumped the last load from my dustpan into the bin and picked up my books from the rack beside the metal lathe. I walked out of the metal shop and into the hallway. Crowds of students were scrambling past in both directions, anxious to get the weekend under way. I started down the hall and thought about just leaving, not going to Rolands office at all, just taking off out the front door and letting whatever was going to hit the fan wait until Monday. But just as I had my hand on the panic bar of the door, I changed my mind. Putting Roland off would only make things worse. I would be making him twice as angry and giving him one more thing to stack up against me.

I turned around at the door and headed down the long hallway, past the biology and chemistry labs, toward Roland's office. In a classroom across from the bio lab, I noticed the dance committee: a group of students bent over Bristol board signs with magic markers in their hands. One girl stood apart from the rest. She held a rolled streamer in her hand and was pulling at its wrapper to open it. It was Sonya Bates. She had been in my class the year before, and I had not seen her since then, though I knew she had just been elected senior class president that week. She was wearing a white blouse and blue skirt that showed the full outlines of her body. She had long black hair that hung down over her shoulders. Her skin was a delicate, even white. She was looking at the streamer in her hands as though what she would do with it were deathly important. It was a way she had of looking at things that I had noticed the year before. Everything was important to her.

She looked up from the streamer and smiled at me. I looked away quickly and continued down the hall.

Roland wanted to talk to me about a window. Someone had broken one near the side entrance of the school. This sounded like something I might have done, but of course I denied it. There was nothing to be gained from telling Roland the truth: that I didn't know whether or not I had broken the window. I honesdy didn't think I had, but I couldn't say one hundred percent for sure. I was doing many things in the space of a week back then, and I did not feel completely in control of them all. Roland would have thought that a weak answer, one that implied guilt, and I could understand that point of view easily enough. Anyone who hadn't done something as deliberate and destructive as kicking out a window should know he had not done it. So I gave him the probable answer: No. Absolutely. I had not broken the window.

Roland wasn't going to press the point with me, I could tell that. It wasn't like him to call me into his office and accuse me outright of anything he couldn't prove. If he suspected I had done something, his method was to ask me what I knew about it. "What do you know about the egg stains on the curtains in the gym?" for example. So even though he did not accuse me of breaking the window, did not come out and say I had done it, I knew I was being accused.

I sat in Roland's office and ground my teeth. I dug my fingernails into the cheap upholstery of the seat. I was angry at myself because of the pledge I had made to stay out of trouble. The pledge was barely a week old, and already I had blown it. But I was also angry at Roland for accusing me of something because of who I was, and because of things I had done before. There was no evidence against me: I was guilty by association with my own past.

Roland was a big, square, stocky man with pale skin and kinky, jet-black hair. His jaw was covered with a curly black beard. His lips, his moustache, and the tip of his nose were stained a dull orange from nicotine. When he opened his mouth you could see where he had cleaned the nicotine stains from his front teeth.

"Let me just tell you this," Roland said. Smoke rose thick about his head and rubbed against the dull walls of his office. He butted a cigarette in an ashtray on his desk. "Let me just tell you about my new policy on you." He threw back his head and blew out a last breath of smoke.

"You got a whole policy just on me," I said.

"Well, it's a policy, and it applies in this case," he said.

"I don't know what case you're talking about," I said. "I didn't do anything."

He looked at me seriously, like a banker might look at a businessman on TV. "Just hear me out," he said. "This has important ramifications for you." He folded his hands on the desk in front of him. "Look at this office," he said.

I looked around. It was just a closet with a window.

"How many times have you been in here in the last few years?"

I opened my mouth to answer.

He raised his hands. "No. No," he said. "Don't answer. Just think for once. Think of how many times you might have been in here."

I thought. How many times had I been in his office? I did not know, but it was a high number.

"Do you know there are students in this school who have never seen the inside of this room?" he said. "That must be a strange thought to you. That must be like trying to think of life before TV."

He had me. It did strike me as odd. Someone who had not been in the principal's office!

He pointed to his ashtray. "There are students," he said, "who do not know I smoke."

I laughed. Everyone knew he smoked. Smoking was prohibited in most parts of the school, but you could smell it off Roland a mile away, off his clothes and his breath. We called him Mr. Horse-shit-breath.

"Okay, laugh," he said. His face turned pale. The tops of his ears began to burn red. "Laugh. But you haven't heard the funny part yet." He smiled at me. "The funny part is," he said, "the funny part is, you will never see the inside of this office again." He paused a moment. I felt my chest tightening. He knew he had my attention now.

"You see this?" he said. He lifted a sheet of paper from the top of his desk. The school crest was printed at the top of the page. The school motto appeared beside the crest: *Prudens Futuri.* Typed on the paper, neatly spaced and numbered, were the school's rules of conduct. It was a system of demerit points. You got one point if a teacher reported that you were unprepared for class, three points if you were reported late. For fighting you got fifteen points. When you had accumulated fifteen points, you were suspended for three days. If you were over sixteen, which I was, and you got suspended more than once, which I had already been, they could throw you out for good.

"I see it," I said.

"You know this off by heart," he said. He tore the paper

in two and dropped it into his waste basket. "No more," he said. "I'm not going to trouble myself with rules any more." He stood up and reached across to the edge of the desktop near me. A smell of tobacco, toothpaste, and instant coffee came from his mouth. "You fuck up once more," he said, "and you're gone. I'll come up with the reasons later."

My heart was racing.

"I'm sick of looking at you," he said. He pointed to the door. "Get out."

After talking to Roland, my idea was to get away from things. I had made this promise to myself less than a week before: the promise to keep my nose clean. And here I was in the thick of it already. The principal had used the f-word with me! I felt disgusted and confused.

I waited inside the school until most of the other kids had cleared away from the front of the building. Some members of the dance committee were still working on posters, but I didn't see Sonya anywhere. When there were only a couple of students standing before the front door, I went out and walked straight home. I sat for a while at the kitchen table, holding my head in my hands. I thought of making myself some Kraft Dinner, but by the time that would be ready my mother or father might be back, and I did not want to face either of them.

The phone rang. It was Rick Patterson. Rick and I were the only two boys from the Red Row in all of grade eleven. Rick was a year younger than me. Grade eleven was where he was supposed to be.

"Jimmy," Rick said.

"Don't call me Jimmy," I said.

"Okay, okay," he said. "Jim. Christ!" He cleared his throat.

"Never saw you after school."

"That's funny," I said. "I never saw you either."

"Anyways." He cleared his throat again. "Bunch of us are going up the cut tonight. Before the dance. Whaddya want to drink?"

"I ain't going," I said.

"Why?" he said.

"Because I just ain't going." I hung up the phone, went upstairs to my parents' bedroom, and took ten dollars from the Bible on the dresser, where my mother kept the milk money.

I walked up Foord Street and stood a while across from the liquor commission. People were coming and going now. The work week was over. Cars moved up and down the street. People were collecting their mail at the post office before they went home. Down in front of Chuck Wagon Pizza a steady stream of customers went in and out the door, carrying take-out pizza to their idling cars.

I eyed the crowd that swarmed in front of the liquor store. There was an art to knowing who would go in for you. Generally it was younger people. People who looked at you as you stood there, waiting for you to ask. The first person I approached went in for me, a man with an Antigonish accent. I gave him my mother's ten dollars and went behind the store to wait for him. When he came out of the store and around the corner into the parking lot, he handed me a six-pack of Alexander Keith's India Pale Ale.

"Those who like it, like it a lot, kid," he said, quoting the TV commercial and pretending not to be nervous. His hand shook a little as he gave me my change. He looked over his shoulder quickly and said, "You forget my face quick."

I put my fingers into the handle in the box and said, "That shouldn't be hard to do." I turned my back on him and left the parking lot. But for some reason I did not forget that man's face. Though I have never seen him again, I would recognize him instantly if I did. He was short and stocky with a thick waist and wide shoulders. His face was short and broad. He had thick lips, a small nose, and round, chubby cheeks. He was a young man, in his early twenties, but he was almost bald, with only a thin blond fringe above his ears. The beginnings of a double chin stuck up over his shirt collar.

With the beer tucked under my arm, I headed for the outskirts of town. I passed through the main street, turned down Acadia Avenue, crossed the railyard, and walked downhill through a narrow field to a stand of alders. A narrow path twisted through the alders to the west bank of the East River. I followed the rocky bank upstream to a spot where the river bent and got wide, the water rippling out over a bed of rocks. I stuck the box of beer in the water and pulled out my first one warm.

I sat on a log a short distance back from the bank, sipping the warm beer and marvelling at the river, at the way it flowed. The way it rolled over and around everything in its path. I could see Plymouth Bridge from where I sat, Plymouth Park at the far end of it.

In the field directly across from me, cows made their noise. A man came out of the house there — the farmer, I guessed — and went into a big barn. The cows did not look up at him, but they knew it was time. They gathered together in a group in a corner of the pasture and formed a line into the barn. A long time later the farmer came out of the barn and went back into the house.

When the sun had gone down and the last glint of light had drained from the sky, I could no longer see the river, but I listened to it. The sky overhead was clear, and the stars burned their tiny holes in the dark. Now and again the headlights of a car crossed the bridge, and the rattle of tires on planks made a thumping noise. The lights in the farmhouse, and in the houses nearby, shone across to me. I wondered what it must be like to be a farmer, to have a piece of the earth that was your own, and to understand exactly what you had to do.

I thought about the people in the houses of Plymouth Park, and wondered what you did in life that led to your owning a house, raising a family, having neighbours. I wondered if any of those people had ever broken a window that was not their own. I wondered if anyone had ever had reason to suspect them of something, not for what they had done, but simply for who they were. I wondered if they had ever come to the riverbank and drunk beer. It occurred to me, looking across the river and thinking about the people in the houses there, that I had lived my whole life within a mile of Plymouth Park, but I did not know a soul who lived there. It might have been a different planet.

The dance had been going for about an hour by the time I climbed the hill at Jubilee Avenue and stood at the far end of the lawn in front of the gym. Roland was having a smoke on the stairs that led up to the gym door. He bent his head over his cigarette to take a drag, then leaned back and exhaled into the air above him.

Through the glass doors behind Roland, two girls sat at a table. A money box lay open before them. Roland finished his cigarette and went back inside. He started talking to Ms. Whalley, a chemistry teacher. The music pounded. The glass in the doors shook. Beyond Roland and Whalley and the girls at the table, lights flashed. The dance floor pulsed with silhouettes. I could see the shadow of the DJ up on the stage.

A car pulled into the parking lot, and four grade ten boys got out. I pulled my ball cap down over my eyes, crouched down a bit, so I would not stand out too tall, and fell in behind them as they walked through the door.

The music hit me in the face when I stepped inside. Roland spoke over it. "Well, this is it," he said.

I froze.

Roland turned away from Whalley. He looked in my direction. I shrank down behind the guy ahead of me. I knew I smelled of beer, and if Roland came near, that was all he would need.

I breathed through my nose. Roland crooked his neck a bit and peered out the glass door behind me. "This is it," he said again. "Fall. It's black out already." He turned back to Ms. Whalley. I quickly paid my two dollars and waited until I was inside the gym before I sighed with relief.

Two double rows of dancing bodies, boys on one side, girls on the other, stretched lengthwise from one end of the gym to the other. Here and there stood groups of five to ten boys, or five to ten girls.

I walked the circumference of the gym to get an idea of who was there. About halfway, someone grabbed my shoulder from behind and spun me around. I clenched my fists and braced myself, then relaxed when I saw who it was. Rick Patterson wore jeans and a jean jacket, a Red Sox cap pulled down to his eyebrows. He had a big drunken smile on his face.

"Hey, Jimmy," he said. "How come you never come up the cut, man?"

I moved in close to him. Our chests touched. He stood

a head over me and had a good twenty-five pounds on me in weight.

"Stop calling me Jimmy," I said.

"Hey, man, hey." He showed me the palms of his hands. He stepped back. "Just asking a question."

I looked him in the eye.

"Guess what, man," he said. "Guess what's here."

I was only half listening to him. I scanned the faces in the part of the gym I had not been in.

"A nigger," he said. "From New Glasgow. The one that works at McDonald's. He's here with a McDonald's party."

It did not shock me to hear Rick say *nigger*; that's what almost everybody said. It was not a word I used myself, though. I had been taught better. My father was a union man, and in his day that meant

We are black and white together
We shall not be moved.

I turned away from Rick to check out the rest of the dance.

Between the doors of the Boys and Girls washrooms stood Sonya Bates. She worked weekends at McDonald's and was part of the McDonald's party, boys and girls, who stood in a clump, milling about and socializing.

I walked into her crowd and tapped her on the shoulder. "Hey, Sonya," I said. The whole McDonald's party turned and looked at me.

Sonya looked at her friends, then turned to me.

"Sonya," I said. I took her by the shoulders and tried to twist her away from the crowd so everyone would not hear. She went stiff in my hands and would not turn. I pushed in close to her.

"You feel like dancing?" I said.

She backed away from me, fanning her hand through the air. "You've been drinking," she said.

The McDonald's people laughed. They smiled at Sonya. People nearby turned to look at what was happening.

I walked into the bathroom. The door closed behind me and deadened the noise from outside.

I looked at myself in the mirror over the sink and punched the paper towel dispenser. "Damn!" I said. I shook my hand in the air. Blood oozed from all four knuckles. I had to push my other thumb under the fingers to uncurl them. The knuckle of my middle finger was back about two centimetres from where it should have been. The paper towel machine was smeared with blood. There was a big dent in its cover.

I heard a noise and looked into the mirror. Behind the reflection of my face was the guy Rick had told me about. The black guy. He was coming out of one of the toilet stalls. I held my damaged fist and looked at him. He looked back.

His name was Charles Borden. We had played hockey against each other, but I did not really know him. Apart from our contact on the ice, I knew his name and he probably knew mine. Recently I had noticed him in the kitchen at McDonalds in New Glasgow, running back and forth between machines.

Borden had two or three inches on me in height, and he was slender, but in no way skinny. He had a frame. You could tell that it would take something to knock him over.

"What are *you* doing here?" I said.

His back stiffened. He shook his shoulders a little. "Just having a shit, man," he said. He tried a smile.

"Stop joking with me," I said. I turned from the mirror.

His smile disappeared. "McDonald's party," he said. He looked at the door.

"McDonald's party!" I said. I filled my lungs with air.

His eyes widened for a moment, then went back to normal. He looked to the door again.

My hand started to throb. I let out my breath, turned to the sink, and ran water over my knuckles. The music got loud, then soft again, as Borden opened the door and went out.

I pulled a length of paper towel from the dispenser and dried my hands, then threw the towel into the garbage and entered one of the toilet stalls, closing the door behind me.

The music got loud, then deadened again. A nervous feeling tingled in my stomach. I waited a long time in the stall. The music stayed muted. The door to the dance floor did not open again. Whoever was standing out there was waiting for me.

I flipped the latch on the stall door and stepped out.

Roland was leaning against a sink, his arms folded over his chest. I pushed my bad hand into my pocket.

"Who did this?" Roland said. He pointed a thumb at the towel dispenser.

"Did what?" I said. I held up my good hand. I took a step toward the door.

"Don't be funny," he said.

I took another step.

"Let me smell your breath," he said.

"Let me smell yours," I said, and rushed out the door.

"Stairway to Heaven" was playing. Fewer people were dancing, so the McDonald's crowd had swelled. I shouldered my way through them and bolted for the other side of the gym.

By the time Roland came out of the bathroom, I was crouched against the wall next to a fire exit. Roland scanned the gym. He peered at the dance floor.

I stayed crouched low until I saw him go back to the foyer.

When I stood up, Rick ran to me from the corner. "Roland's hot on your trail," he said. "Are you in shit again or what?"

"Aw, Horse-shit-breath," I said.

"Hey, you know what, man," Rick said. "Guess who Sonya's dancing with."

"Sonya who?" I said.

"Very funny, man," he said. "Nigger boy. That's who."

"What?" I said.

"You heard me," he said. He pointed to a spot on the dance floor near the stage. Sonya and Borden stood embracing each other, moving with the music.

As I walked toward them "Stairway to Heaven" finished and a fast song started. They separated and began dancing farther apart.

I stopped at the stage and leaned back against it, not ten feet from where they were dancing. Rick had followed me and leaned back beside me.

"Get lost," I told him.

"I want to see what happens," he said.

I grabbed the biceps of his closest arm and pushed my fingertips hard into the muscle. "Get lost," I said.

"Ow! Jesus!" he said. He shook his arm from my grip. "What a guy!" He gave me a hurt look and walked away.

Borden and Sonya were dancing, trying not to look at me. I eyed Borden. I made my chest rise and fall as I stood there. I looked at him from slits of eyes.

The next song started, but Borden's and Sonya's movements got stiffer and slower. Borden glanced over at me. He didn't look at my eyes, he looked at my body. He sized me up, then looked around the gym. I knew what he was seeing: white faces, everywhere. He said something to Sonya, and they stopped dancing. He walked away from her and tried to blend into the McDonald's crowd by the bathrooms.

Sonya turned and came toward me. For a hopeless instant I thought she would ask me to dance.

"You asshole!" she hissed.

"Me?" I said. I pointed a finger at my chest.

"Stop it," she said.

"Stop what?" I said. "I don't see me doing nothing." I held up my hands and looked over both my shoulders. "What am I doing?"

She straightened her arms at her sides and rounded her hands into fists.

I smirked at her.

She walked away.

After a moment, I followed her to the McDonald's crowd. The floor was packed now, and all but a few of the McDonald's party were up dancing. Borden stood in the centre of a circle of mostly girls. A few grade nine and ten boys were there, but it was the girls who looked at me. They did not move. Borden checked his breathing, in and out.

I stood on the outskirts of their circle for a moment. I folded my arms.

A voice in my ear said, "Go easy, man." It was Rick. "I just saw a cop come in."

"I thought I told you to get lost," I said.

"Man," he said. "A *cop*."

I pushed through the circle to Borden. Sonya ran for the foyer.

"Hey, hey," Borden said. He held up his hands. His palms were white. A crowd started to gather.

"What are you doing here?" I said. I pushed my chest into his.

"As far as I'm concerned," he said. "I'm at a party."

I grabbed his shoulder and pushed him.

He stepped back a few steps.

I pushed him again. Some buttons flew off his shirt.

"Hey!" he said. He pulled at his collar.

"Shut up," I said. I measured him with a push to the chest, then swung my broken hand at his head. He dodged it and ducked behind me. I turned to face him.

Two hands gripped me from behind. "You're gone," said Fred Roland. "You're out."

I broke his hold and ran for the bathroom. I was half-way out the bathroom window when someone grabbed me by the ankles. I kicked and squirmed and almost fell out the window upside down. "Don't fight me," a voice said. I looked down at my feet and saw that it was a cop who had me. "Don't fight me," the cop said again.

"Okay," I said. "Okay, okay." I climbed down from the window ledge.

"You're out of my hair now," Roland was saying. He grinned at me.

"Horse-shit-breath!" I said. I moved to kick at him.

The cop clamped my arm hard. "Ow!" I said. "Jesus!"

"I'm taking you out of here," the cop said. "You don't mess around and I won't have to put the cuffs on you." He pulled me back from the window and stopped in front of the sinks.

"You got me," I said. I held up my free hand. Roland was still smiling. I looked into the mirror and saw the dark look on my face.

The music was going when we came out of the bathroom. A small crowd was waiting for us outside the door, but most people were still dancing. The cop led me across the gym to the foyer. Behind the money table stood Sonya and Borden. They were talking to Ms. Whalley. Ms. Whalley nodded her head gravely. I stopped before the door and looked across at Borden. His eyes met mine. His hair was in a tight afro and clipped short. He had a wide forehead, broad cheek-bones, and a narrow chin. The crook in the bridge showed where his nose had been broken pretty badly at one time.

The cop twisted my arm and shoved me forward. I turned my head to keep looking at Borden. As Borden looked at me, a row of lines spread across his forehead, but otherwise his expression was blank and did not change.

"You fucking nigger," I said. He did not move or flinch.

The cop pushed me outside. "No trouble," he said. "No trouble, now." He led me down the walkway to the parking lot and put me in the back seat of his cruiser. The first thing I noticed was that there were no handles on the insides of the cruiser's doors. There was a cage across the top of the seat before me, to make sure I couldn't make a play for the cop.

So this is where I belong, I thought, in the back seat of a car like this.

At that time of night the cop and I were the only ones in the police station. The tile floor in the room where we stood gleamed under a fresh coat of wax. A faint smell of cigarette smoke came from the walls and furniture.

The cop fined me thirteen dollars and fifty cents for drinking under age. When I told him I couldn't pay it, he made me sign a form that said I'd pay before the end of the month. After I'd signed, he put two copies of the form in a file folder on the desk and handed me the original. He looked down at the floor for a moment and chewed his lip like he was thinking of something to say.

"Look," he said at last. "What are you doing?"

I smirked at him and shook my head. "This is kid's stuff," I said.

"That's where it starts," he said. "Kid's stuff."

I shrugged. "I don't know," I said.

"You don't know," he said. "I'm telling you — " He thought a moment, then waved a hand in the air. "To hell with it," he said.

He led me down a hallway to a small, brightly lit office. He motioned to a wooden armchair, and I sat in it.

"Just sit still for a while," he said, then he went out the door.

I sat slumped in the chair, half asleep. I looked down at my broken hand. The middle knuckle was pushed back. The flesh over it was swollen. The skin was turning black.

I thought the cop might be phoning my father to come and get me. That's one thing I knew sometimes happened in these cases. I sat in the office with my hand throbbing, waiting for my father to come through the door. But at 12:30, a half hour after the dance was scheduled to let out, he let me go.

"You go straight the Jesus home," he said.

"No problem there," I said.

Outside, the night had become cool. I could see my breath. I looked overhead, but no stars showed beyond the streetlights. I went to the Quik Pik store and spent the last of my mother's ten dollars on a microwave donair, which I ate on the way home.

It was about a year later that I saw Charles Borden again, after a hockey game I'd gone to see in New Glasgow. I was walking out of the rink alone as he came in with a group of maybe seven friends.

He looked at me. My heart raced. My throat tightened. He looked away.

This is what happened. At the time, nothing about this incident bothered me at all. I did not think twice about what I had done, or what had happened to me or anyone else as a result. The life I had been leading as a student had ended, and a new life had started for me: the life of someone who has been thrown out of school. As far as I could see, that was all there was to it.

But now, as distant from that time and place as I am, I wonder about these events in my life and what they mean. Where would I be now if I had stayed in school? Why did I call that kid that name? I know now that Borden could have pounded shit out of me, if not at the dance in Albion Mines, then at the rink in New Glasgow. Why didn't he?

Sometimes I will be walking down a street in Saskatoon, or Montreal, or Vancouver, or wherever time and circumstance have brought me, and I will stop dead where I stand. My skin will go cold. The hair on my arms will stand on end. A single drop of sweat will bead down the ridge of my spine. Charles Borden's face will flash in my mind, and I will have to shake my head to get rid of the picture.

I don't know why I did what I did. Maybe it was the time and place. But nothing anywhere has changed.

• ACKNOWLEDGEMENTS

Any person engaged in the creation of works that through incessantly striving for perfection, he or she hopes someday to call artistic, owes much to many. It would be an exaggeration to say that this book owes something to everyone I've ever met, but it would not be a gross exaggeration. The following merit special mention.

For support, Kathy Hughes. For friendship and advice, Michael Keezing, *il miglior fabbro*. For encouragement, the Department of Creative Writing, University of British Columbia, especially Jerry, George, and Brian. The Sage Hill Writing Experience, especially Jane, Jill, Larry, Joan, and Darlene. For recognition and editorial counsel, Martha Sharpe.

Special thanks also go to several people I have never met. They are: For light, Raymond Carver. For warmth, Peter Gzowski, and the entire CBC Radio network. For fire, Stanislaw Lem.

Leo McKay, Jr. was born in Stellarton, Nova Scotia and teaches English in Truro, Nova Scotia. His short story collection *Like This* was shortlisted for the Giller Prize, and his first novel, *Twenty-Six* won the 2004 Dartmouth Book Award.

LIST

The A List

The Outlander · Gil Adamson

The Circle Game · Margaret Atwood

Survival · Margaret Atwood

The Hockey Sweater and Other Stories · Roch Carrier

Roch Carrier's La Guerre Trilogy · Roch Carrier

Queen Rat · Lynn Crosbie

The Honeyman Festival · Marian Engel

Eleven Canadian Novelists Interviewed by Graeme Gibson · Graeme Gibson

Five Legs · Graeme Gibson

De Niro's Game · Rawi Hage

Kamouraska · Anne Hébert

Ticknor · Sheila Heti

No Pain Like This Body · Harold Sonny Ladoo

Civil Elegies · Dennis Lee

Ana Historic · Daphne Marlatt

Like This · Leo McKay Jr.

The Selected Short Fiction of Lisa Moore · Lisa Moore

Alden Nowlan Selected Poems · Alden Nowlan

Poems For All the Annettes · Al Purdy

This All Happened · Michael Winter